Praise for
the Blood Coven Vampire Novels

"Delightful, surprising, and engaging."
　　　　—Rachel Caine, *New York Times* bestselling author

"Dark, delicious, and full of surprises."
　　　　—Heather Brewer, *New York Times* bestselling author

Night School

"An action-packed story with appealing characters, dark humor, and a new spin on both the worlds of the undead and the fae . . . Will appeal to adult fans of *Buffy the Vampire Slayer* as well as the Harry Potter series and the Twilight novels."　　　　　　　　　　　—*Library Journal*

"*Night School* is another thrilling installment to Rayne and Sunny's story."　　　　　　　—*Romance Reviews Today*

Bad Blood

"A vampire book so worth reading, with dark humor, distinctive voice, and a protagonist clever enough to get herself out of trouble . . . A great ride."
　　　　—Ellen Hopkins, *New York Times* bestselling author

"Mancusi writes with a wicked sense of humor."
　　　　　　　　　　　　　　　—*Novel Reads*

continued . . .

Girls That Growl

"An amusing teenage vampire tale . . . Young adults will enjoy growling alongside of this vampire slayer who has no time left for homework." —*Midwest Book Review*

"Refreshing . . . different from all of those other vampire stories . . . a very original plot." —*Flamingnet*

Stake That

"A fast-paced story line . . . both humorous and hip . . . A top read!" —*Love Vampires*

"Rayne is a fascinating protagonist . . . readers will want to stake out Mari Mancusi's fun homage to Buffy." —*The Best Reviews*

Boys That Bite

"A wonderfully original blend of vampire/love/adventure drama which teens will find refreshingly different." —*Midwest Book Review*

"Liberal doses of humor keep things interesting . . . and the surprise ending will leave readers bloodthirsty for the next installment of the twins' misadventures with the undead. A ghoulishly fun read." —*School Library Journal*

"Starring two distinct, likable twins, the vampire between them, and a coven of terrific support characters . . . Filled with humor and action . . . insightfully fun." —*The Best Reviews*

BLOOD TIES

MARI MANCUSI

BERKLEY BOOKS, NEW YORK

THE BERKLEY PUBLISHING GROUP
Published by the Penguin Group
Penguin Group (USA) Inc.
375 Hudson Street, New York, New York 10014, USA
Penguin Group (Canada), 90 Eglinton Avenue East, Suite 700, Toronto, Ontario M4P 2Y3, Canada
(a division of Pearson Penguin Canada Inc.)
Penguin Books Ltd., 80 Strand, London WC2R 0RL, England
Penguin Group Ireland, 25 St. Stephen's Green, Dublin 2, Ireland (a division of Penguin Books Ltd.)
Penguin Group (Australia), 250 Camberwell Road, Camberwell, Victoria 3124, Australia
(a division of Pearson Australia Group Pty. Ltd.)
Penguin Books India Pvt. Ltd., 11 Community Centre, Panchsheel Park, New Delhi—110 017, India
Penguin Group (NZ), 67 Apollo Drive, Rosedale, Auckland 0632, New Zealand
(a division of Pearson New Zealand Ltd.)
Penguin Books (South Africa) (Pty.) Ltd., 24 Sturdee Avenue, Rosebank, Johannesburg 2196,
South Africa

Penguin Books Ltd., Registered Offices: 80 Strand, London WC2R 0RL, England

This book is an original publication of The Berkley Publishing Group.

PRINTING HISTORY
Berkley trade paperback edition / August 2011

Library of Congress Cataloging-in-Publication Data

Mancusi, Marianne.
    Blood ties / Mari Mancusi. — Berkley trade pbk. ed.
      p.   cm.
    Summary: As the Blood Coven is gearing up for its toughest fight yet, Sunny McDonald is trying to decide between her vampire boyfriend, Magnus, and Jayden, the human who once saved her life.
    ISBN 978-0-425-24136-3
    [1. Vampires—Fiction. 2. Twins—Fiction. 3. Sisters—Fiction.] I. Title.
    PZ7.M312178Bl   2011
    [Fic]—dc22   2011003893

PRINTED IN THE UNITED STATES OF AMERICA

10 9 8 7 6 5 4 3 2 1

To my agent, Kristin Nelson, and my editor, Kate Seaver, for making the continuation of this series possible. And to the Blood Coven Vampires in Training—who make writing each and every book an exciting, rewarding experience. To the Werearmadillo writing group, for constant support and love. And finally, to all the Jayden fans out there who demanded more of his story—this one's for you!

BLOOD TIES

The World According to Sunshine (Sunny) McDonald . . .

There are a lot of people in this world who want nothing more than to stand out in a crowd. To gain fame and fortune and be recognized wherever they go. They want attention. They want notoriety. And they'll stop at nothing until they have five million followers on Twitter and TMZ has justified the expense of picking up their trail on every Starbucks run.

Which is all fine and good, in theory, anyway. But in the words of the wise old (and oh-so-classy) Pussycat Dolls: "Be careful what you wish for, 'cause you just might get it." And once you do, you may be craving normalcy like a bastard. And there will be nothing you can do to get it back.

I, on the other hand, never wanted to be famous. Or notorious. Or anything "ous," except maybe anonymous. A nondescript face in the crowd. A normal girl living a normal life with a normal job, a normal husband, and 2.3 normal kids playing out behind a normal white picket fence. Maybe we'd have a swimming pool, but that's as wild and crazy as I ever wanted to get.

But no. During the last year, I've learned the hard way that normal just ain't in the cards for me and my family. And, whether I like it or not, I've really got no choice but to let our freak flag fly for all to see.

For those of you just joining us (um, where have you been?!) it all started one night back in May. Back when I thought I *was* normal and my biggest worry was whether the guy I was crushing on knew I even existed. Back then, I still figured the world worked just like they told you in school and the laws of physics, gravity, and mortality applied to everyone—even my crazy twin sister, Rayne, who I decided, stupidly, to accompany on an outing to Club Fang, the local Goth joint, one fateful night.

That night started out good. I met a guy. A really hot one. Unfortunately, things went downhill from there after he mistook me for my vampire-wannabe sister and bit me in the neck, basically turning me into a vampire in a bloody bad case of mistaken identity. I was so not pleased, let me tell you.

You see, turns out, while I had been angling for a prom date and playing field hockey, Rayne had been going to night school classes, getting her vampire certification. The bite was sort of her graduation gift—her passport into the world of the undead. Magnus, the vampire, was supposed to become her blood mate, which is basically like a soul mate kind of thing for vamps, and the two of them were meant to live happily ever after as members of the Blood Coven in a crypt built for two.

Anyway, to make a long story somewhat short, Magnus and I ended up going on this wild adventure to England to find the Holy Grail (yes, the real one!), which evidently was the only thing that could cure me. During this time, we fell in love—go figure—

and have been dating ever since. Not the normal boyfriend I'd hoped to find. But awesome, just the same. (Even though sometimes he can be a total workaholic, which can drive me insane.)

We've had a lot of adventures since then—and pretty much none of them normal. Like when my vampire-wannabe sister found out she was actually destined to become a vampire slayer instead. (Which became useful when the werewolf cheerleaders came to town.) Or when the vampire Jareth she once hated saved her life—and finally made her vampire dreams come true. And then there was the time me and my human friend Jayden managed to stop an evil Las Vegas vampire from destroying the Blood Coven from within. That was pretty amazing—even if it did almost kill both of us.

But, to be honest, the biggest paranormal turning point came not from the vampires at all, but from our very own parents. Our hippie-dippie mom and our absentee dad who, one day, decided to break the news that Rayne and I aren't human at all—but rather full-blooded fairies! Not only that—but fairy princesses— next in line for the Light Court throne.

At that point, I had to kiss normal good-bye for good.

Hiding out from the fairies ended up being an adventure in and of itself—with Rayne and me spending some quality time at Riverdale, a school for vampire slayers deep in the Swiss Alps. That's where Rayne met Corbin, a slayer-in-training who unknowingly fell for her vampire charms. Unfortunately, it wasn't a happily-ever-after kind of love affair and ended with Corbin being turned into a vampire himself. Now he's on the loose somewhere, probably plotting his revenge against the Blood Coven and my sister.

Which brings us to today. Mom's off ruling Fairyland. We just buried our father, may he rest in peace. My sister's going through a twelve-step program at a vampire rehab, trying to get control of her whole bloodlust thing. And an evil fringe group of Slayer Inc. that we uncovered at Riverdale (that calls themselves the Alphas) is determined to create vampiric fae hybrids in a bid to take over the world.

And, as for me? Well, I've just enrolled in Las Vegas High School—which seems like the normal thing to do.

We'll see how long that lasts . . .

1

"Hey, Sunny, over here!"

I look up from stuffing my field hockey stick into my bag, my eyes widening with horror as they fall upon a long, black stretch limousine, pulling up curbside to my new high school, behind the waiting school bus. The window slides down and from inside I can see Magnus, still shadowed in the darkness, beckoning for me to come over. I try to pretend I don't hear him. Don't even know him. So of course that makes him shout even louder. As a rule, former knights in shining armor from medieval times can so not take a hint.

"Oy! Sunny! I'm right here!"

"Whoa, who's the hottie?" whistles Kierra, the field hockey center and one of the only potential friends I've managed to score my first week here at Las Vegas High School. In other words, the

last person on Earth I want to introduce to the Master of the
Blood Coven—one of the largest vampire groups on the Eastern
Seaboard—aka my current boyfriend, Magnus. Who, I might add,
may soon become my *former* boyfriend Magnus if he doesn't pull
away from my high school parking lot in the next five seconds.

Kierra squints to get a better glimpse into the luxurious limo.
I mean, really, Magnus? A freaking limo? Could we get any more
My Super Sweet Sixteen if we tried? These girls are so going to
get the wrong idea about me.

"Wow, Sunny," chimes in Hana, the goalie. "You've been holding out on us!"

Magnus tosses the girls a friendly wave. My only saving grace
is the knowledge that he'll literally catch on fire if he tries to step
out of the car and into the sweltering Vegas sunshine.

"Is he your boyfriend?" Taylar, the midfielder, queries.

I try to send Magnus mental signals to vacate the premises. If
only I had vampire telepathy like Rayne does with Jareth. Then
again, I think she only has the ability to summon her boyfriend
to her, not send him away. Which evidently I don't need special
superpowers to do.

I realize the three girls are staring at me questioningly. "Oh
him?" I stammer. "He's just . . . some guy I know."

"Yeah. Some guy in a *limo!*" Taylar adds. "It's, like, seriously,
so Chuck Bass in *Gossip Girl!*" She pretends to swoon.

"Yeah! And you're like Blair!" gushes Kierra. "Except, you
know, without the designer wardrobe." The three girls study my
tank top and jeans ensemble from Old Navy with critical eyes. I
am so going to kill Magnus. What is he even doing awake this
time of day anyway?

"Hi, Chuck Bass!" coos Hana, running over to the limo and

sticking her head in. She's quickly joined by Taylar and Kierra. "Buy any hotels lately?"

Magnus cocks his head in question. "I'm sorry?"

"Um, he doesn't get out much. I mean, stay in much," I interject, running to the car and pushing them aside. "I mean, he doesn't watch a lot of TV."

"Actually I do quite enjoy *The Vampire Diaries*," Magnus interjects with a sly smile.

Oh. My. God.

The field hockey players *squee* in unison, squeezing past me, their heads all trying to fit through the limo window at once.

"Want to come hang with us?" Hana asks.

"We're going to crash the Mandalay pool to catch some rays," adds Kierra.

"And no offense, man, but you sure look like you can use some," teases Taylar playfully.

"I appreciate your offer, ladies," Magnus says grandly. "But I must regretfully decline. Perhaps another day, or night, I mean, after the sun goes down?"

Okay that's it. I'm done. I push through the blockade of girls and yank open the limo door. "Sorry, they're busy," I reply, before any of them can answer. I dive into the limo and slam the door shut behind me. "See you guys tomorrow!" I cry, stabbing at the window button, praying it will move faster the more times I press it.

"Can we, like, go?" I bite at the chauffeur as I watch my new friends try to squint through the one-way glass. Luckily the guy obliges and we pull out of the school parking lot at long last. Excellent. Now I can at least die of embarrassment off of school property.

"Sunny?" I realized Magnus is staring at me questioningly.

I turn to him. "What the hell was that, Magnus?" I demand.

"What was what?" he asks innocently. "I just thought you'd like a ride home."

"Yeah. In a school bus. Or a normal car. Not a stretch limo. Do you know what they're going to think of me now?" I can just imagine them texting their friends as we speak. Three days at my new school and I'm already going to be limo girl with the bad wardrobe.

"I'm sorry, Sunny," Magnus replies, sounding slightly amused. "But limos are just easier for me to get around in during the day." He pauses, then adds, "Next time I'll bring the Jag."

Argh. I flop back in my seat, so giving up.

"What's wrong?"

"What's wrong?" I repeat. "Hmm, I don't know, Magnus. How about the fact that I'm starting a new school and I'm trying to make friends and fit in. That's not easy to do when my vampire boyfriend shows up with a limo and starts talking all weird to my friends."

"Come on," he cajoles. "I thought vampires were all the rage with high school girls these days."

I glower at him. "Only if they sparkle."

Magnus starts laughing at this. I try to frown, to keep being mad, but I have to admit, it is kind of funny. And soon I find myself giggling alongside of him.

"Am I forgiven then?" he asks fondly, looking at me with his beautiful emerald eyes.

I grunt. "Oh, I suppose." I curl into his cool body, rejoicing at the feel of his long, lean frame pressed up against me. After all those lonely nights at Riverdale Academy, aka Slay School, I can't resist a little cuddle from the guy every now and then. Even if he does refuse to follow orders to stay away from my high school.

"Sorry," I say sheepishly. "I know you meant well. It's just . . . I'm in a weird situation, you know? Going to a new school, trying to get people to like me . . ."

"Who *wouldn't* like you?" Magnus asks, planting a kiss on my freckled nose. "You're perfect."

"You're prejudiced."

"Maybe so." He tosses his head arrogantly. "But I've also had a thousand years' experience to draw from. These girls you're trying to impress? They've got seventeen, eighteen, tops."

I can't help but giggle. "So you're saying in a thousand years of searching, you've never found a girl as perfect as me?"

"Vampire's honor," he says, holding his fingers up in Boy Scout pose. Then he grabs me and pulls me close to him, kissing me hungrily on the mouth. I kiss him back, enjoying the feel of his soft lips moving against my own. It's so good to have him back in my arms. I just pray he doesn't have to leave again.

"So, I may have to leave again," he announces suddenly, pulling away from the kiss.

"What? Why?"

He slumps back in his seat. "The Consortium may have found a lead as to where the Alpha Slayers are hiding out. The House Speaker, Pyrus, has requested my presence to help with the investigation." He makes a face. Ever since Pyrus took over as House Speaker of the Consortium, he's seemed determined to make Magnus's life as difficult as possible. And this seems no exception.

"Isn't that more like Jareth's job? You know, the hands-on kind of stuff? No offense, baby, but you're more politician than warrior."

He scowls. "Um, former knight in shining armor, remember?" he says, patting his chest. "And in any case, Jareth's coming along, too. In fact, the majority of coven leaders are mobilizing for this. It's just too big a risk to be taken lightly. Especially now that Corbin's stolen some valuable information from the Blood Coven that can be used against us."

Corbin. The slayer my sister almost drained dry when suffering from blood addiction back at Riverdale Academy. Jareth saved him by turning him into a vampire. But let's just say the guy wasn't so grateful for the favor, seeing as now he's basically turned into the very monster he's so desperate to eliminate from the planet.

"Okay then," I say, gearing up for the challenge. I guess normal high school life will have to be put on hold once again. "Let's swing by the house and I'll pack a bag."

Magnus frowns.

"What?" I ask.

"Sunny, you're not coming."

"Um, excuse me?" Is he for real?

"It's going to be war," Magnus reminds me. "It's too dangerous for you."

"Hello, Magnus!" I wave to him. "Fairy princess, remember? No longer the fragile human girl you need to protect from harm? I want to help."

But my boyfriend just shakes his head. "I don't think it's a good idea, Sunny. If anything were to happen to you, I'd never forgive myself. Not to mention, just having you there would be . . . a distraction."

I stare at him, mouth agape. I can't believe it. Once again I'm being shut out.

"Look, Sun, I'm not trying to be a jerk here . . ."

"Well, then you're failing miserably," I retort. "Driver, stop the car. I'm going to walk the rest of the way!" The driver slows down.

"No!" Magnus corrects. "Keep going." The driver sighs, then speeds up again.

As if that's going to stop me. "Fine, have it your way." I press the button to open the skylight, then push my head through. I can hear Magnus protesting below as I crawl out the window, unfurl my wings out the sides of my tank top, flutter off the moving vehicle, and float down onto the nearby sidewalk, leaving my sun-allergic boyfriend stuck in the car, trying desperately to close the skylight.

Fairies one, vampires zilch.

"Sunny!" Magnus cries furiously, banging on the window. I ignore him, instead addressing the group of tourists that has gathered, gawking at my wings. I give them a little bow before stuffing them back under my shirt. *(Just another Vegas freak here, people, nothing to see!)* Then I storm off down the street heading toward my family's high-rise condo just off the Strip.

"Stay at home, Sunny," I mutter under my breath. "It's way too dangerous, Sunny." I'm so sick of everyone thinking I'm the weak one. After all, no one ever says stuff like that to Rayne. As an official vampire slayer, not to mention an actual vampire, she goes on death-defying adventures for a living. (Yes, I know, I know—a vampire who works as a vampire slayer—seems like a conflict of interest, right? Luckily she's only assigned to take out the bad vamps who don't follow the rules.) But as for me, I might as well be made of freaking glass, according to Magnus and the rest of the sorry vampire race.

It's so unfair.

I walk down an alley through a shortcut off the Strip. About halfway through I wonder if I've made a wise choice. The shadows in the dark seem to claw at me menacingly and I keep hearing strange catlike mews echoing through the air. I wrap my arms around my body and pick up the pace.

A loud clattering makes me jump out of my skin. I whirl around, my eyes catching movement in the darkness. A shadow that can only be human.

"Who's there?" I demand. "Stay back! I've got Mace and I know how to use it." I don't really, of course. But I do have some fairy powers to unfurl if push comes to shove.

"S-S-Sunny?" a weak but familiar voice cries. "Is that really you?"

"Jayden?" I exclaim, rushing toward the shadow, shocked beyond belief. What's he doing here?

I stop short as my eyes fall upon the figure on the ground. While it's definitely Jayden—my best Vegas friend and maybe something more—at the same time he looks . . . wrong somehow. Scarily skinny, all bones and sinew, his eyes are black and hollow-looking and his mouth is bloodstained. I realize in horror he's holding something furry and dead and half-eaten in his hands.

"Oh my God!" I cry. "What happened to you?"

He looks up with pitiful, scared eyes. "Sunny," he whimpers. "You've got to help me. I think . . . I think I might have been turned into a vampire."

2

My first thought is to move him—to drag him somewhere—somewhere safe. But then I see he's trapped himself on a small island of shadow, surrounded by an ocean of sunshine, squinting up at me with pale, bloodshot eyes. New vampires are less sensitive to the sun than fully mature ones—they won't spontaneously combust into flames like the ancient ones do—but I know from personal experience the rays can still hurt like crazy and give you one hell of a sunburn.

My second thought is to call for help. But I realize, too late, that in my haste to make a grand exit, I left the book bag containing my cell phone in Magnus's limo.

So instead I squat down next to him, trying to ignore the rank smell of rotting garbage coming from the Dumpster a few feet away, and wrap my arm around his shoulders, pulling his shivering body against my own. It's like grabbing onto a supersize icicle, and I wonder wildly if my tongue would stick to his skin if I tried to lick him.

"Oh, Jayden, what happened?" I ask, my voice breaking at seeing him in this condition. He clings to me too tightly, as if desperate to absorb my warmth. I squeeze him even tighter, rubbing his back, feeling his spine jutting out from under his thin skin. What's wrong with him? Could he really be infected? He was fine when I saw him a couple weeks before. Recovering nicely from his run-in with Cornelius, healthy enough, even, to take over the leading role in the *Dracula* musical at the Sun Casino.

So how did he go from playing a creature of the night to becoming one in reality? I mean, I've heard of life imitating art, but this seems a bit extreme . . .

"I don't know," he confesses. "I felt fine when I was originally released from the hospital. Just went about my business, taking care of the animals by day and acting in the show by night." He looks up at me, an accusing flicker in his otherwise hollow eyes. "I thought you'd gone back to Massachusetts."

My heart pangs guiltily. Of course he had. And I hadn't exactly done anything to make him think otherwise, either. Sure, I'd been meaning to call him the moment I got back to Vegas from my adventure in Fairyland, but somehow I kept finding reasons to put off the call. Or pick up the phone when I recognized his number on the caller ID, for that matter. So much had happened—so much of my life had changed—so completely—that, to be honest, it was easier to avoid a conversation altogether than to figure out a place to even start.

And now, here in this alleyway, with Jayden fighting for his mortal life, the whole "Sorry, I was busy getting kidnapped by fairies" excuse sounds lamer than "The dog ate my homework."

"It's okay," Jayden adds, his voice laced with bitterness. "I know your boyfriend probably discouraged you keeping in touch."

He wasn't wrong. While Magnus had never specifically spelled out the idea that he didn't want me hanging out with Jayden anymore, I knew he believed no good could come out of a friendship with a guy who clearly liked me as more than a friend.

If only Magnus knew the truth: that I'd been fully prepared to dump him and run away with Jayden. And that it was Jayden himself who talked me into giving Magnus another chance. Maybe then he'd have more respect for the guy . . .

I force my thoughts back to the present. "But then you started feeling weird?" I ask, urging him to continue as I attempt to swallow down the floodwaters of guilt rising to my throat. If only I'd checked in on him. Answered his calls. I am seriously the worst friend ever.

He nods. "The light started bothering my eyes. And then I found it almost impossible to get up in the morning and go to sleep at night. But the biggest change was with the animals." He stares down at the ground sorrowfully. "Now when I enter the room, they all freak out. The dogs start howling uncontrollably. The cats hiss in fear. Sweet little Rex even tried to bite me." His voice chokes on the little wire-haired terrier's name. "I eventually had to quit. My presence was stressing them out so much, they couldn't concentrate on the show."

My heart breaks for him. Poor Jayden. He'd devoted his entire life to working with the rescue dog and cat performers at the Comedy Pet Theater. I remember going backstage with him just weeks ago and seeing the affection in his eyes as he showed off his beloved animals. And, it was clear to me at the time that they loved him as much as he did them.

But that was the mortal him. Pets, as a rule, don't take too kindly to vampires. Something about the smell. Dead meat walking around. Most cats find it confusing. Most dogs simply want a taste.

"After that, everything became a blur," Jayden continues. "I'd have blackouts, wake up somewhere and not remember how I got there or what I'd done. I was starving, but couldn't keep down any food. I started to lose weight like crazy and then this horrible sickness came over me. Like the worst flu I've ever had. I tried to crawl to the hospital, but never made it that far. I've been here in this alleyway for the last three days, I think. I'm losing track. I'm so weak. So hungry. And all I can think of"—he makes a face—"is blood."

I swallow hard. This is not good. "But I don't understand," I say, trying to make sense of his story while at the same time moving away from the topic of drinking blood. "I mean, it's not like vampirism has suddenly gone airborne or anything. You would have had to literally drink vampire blood—or have it injected into you somehow—to become a vampire. But obviously you would remember something like that . . ."

A flicker of fear crosses his face. "Cornelius," he murmurs. "I think maybe some of his blood must have mixed with mine when he bit me."

My heart sinks at his words, remembering all too well the night Jayden saved my life—and the entire Blood Coven—by risking his own. Could he have really somehow become infected while facing off with the evil vampire? 'Cause that would make this whole thing my fault.

"Sunny, please, you've got to help me," Jayden begs. He clutches at my skin with desperate, bluish fingers. Sighing, I wrap him into a hug, pulling him against me, feeling the tears break free from my eyes as he buries his face in my shoulder. If I somehow did this to him—dragged this sweet, innocent boy into my dark world—I don't know how I'm ever going to be able to forgive myself.

"I'm so hungry," he murmurs. "So scared."

"I know," I say, attempting to soothe him with soft murmurs. "I was once bitten by a vampire, too. I know how horrible the transformation can be."

I shudder, remembering that awful week. The pain, the confusion, the wild changes. Of course, at least for me, I had my sister at my side. And Magnus, too, guiding me every step of the way. Jayden has had to go through this whole nightmare alone. With no hope or help. I can't even imagine what that must be like.

"But you're *not* a vampire now," Jayden says, looking up at me. "So could this whole thing still be reversible somehow?" I can hear the thin shred of hope in his voice and it breaks my heart all over again. "Is there still a chance for me to go back to being human?"

I bite my lower lip. That is the $64,000 question, isn't it? "I'm not sure," I hedge. "For me, it took a drop of blood from the Holy Grail."

Jayden's eyes widen. "The Holy—" He shakes his head. "Does that even really exist outside of Monty Python movies?"

"Oh yeah. It exists." I nod. "But it's not like some prescription drug you can have called in to a pharmacy. It's hidden away, deep underground in England and closely guarded by this ancient druid sect. Not exactly as accessible as a Big Gulp at your local 7-Eleven," I add wryly. "Magnus took me there when I was infected and paid off the druids so they would allow me a tiny sip. Of course, I had to drink it within seven days of being bitten.

If you were really infected by Cornelius, well, that would have happened, like, a month ago. So I'm not sure that would even be an option for you."

Though . . .

Inspiration hits me with the force of a ten-ton truck. Technically speaking, I've still got traces of *ye olde Grail blood* swimming through my mortal veins. For full-blooded vampires, this is a total turnoff—and maybe even poisonous. But for a newbie like Jayden—well, maybe he could get some real mortal benefits by taking a sip or two . . .

I bite my lower lip, trying to come to terms with the idea. I've been bitten twice in my life. Once to turn me into a vampire, once to make me mortal again. And let's just say I'm sooo not one of those fang-banger types—like my sister—who totally gets off on the whole thing. (Rayne makes it sound orgasmic. To me, it's—literally—a big pain in the neck.) But still, I got Jayden into this mess. It's my responsibility to get him out—if I can.

And maybe, just maybe, I can.

"Okay, Jayden," I say, reluctantly sweeping my long, dirty blond hair away from my neck. I suck in a breath; I just know I'm going to regret this. But what choice do I have? I can't just leave him here. "Let's try something."

His eyes widen in a mixture of fear and desire. "I don't know, Sunny," he says worriedly and I can see his hard swallow. "I don't want . . ."

But he does want. I can see the hunger in his hollow face. The shaky hands, the bated breath. He wants me badly, even if he can't admit it aloud.

"It's okay," I assure him, trying to sound confident. "I want you to. The Grail blood inside me might make you better. And that's what's important here."

He nods slowly, as if unable to speak. His lips part and my heart breaks all over again as I see his tiny, pointed fangs slide into view. Poor Jayden never asked for this. I just hope we're not too late to save him.

"Bite me," I whisper. And weirdly, I actually want him to. In fact, my whole body is humming with anticipation of the act. Is it his vampire scent—the pheromones given off by creatures of the night—that are seducing my senses? Or is just Jayden himself— the sweetest boy in the world—who has me all turned on?

He cocks his head to the side awkwardly, trying to get in position. I stretch my neck out to give him better access. He leans forward and I can feel his shaky breath on my skin a moment before that all-too-familiar sting.

Ohhh! My eyes roll back in my head as he takes that first, tentative suck—unexpected ecstasy sweeping over me in a tidal wave of emotion. Suddenly I realize that though Magnus has technically bitten me twice, both times he only transferred blood into me. Never took any out.

This feels different. Wayyyy different.

Jayden grabs me by the shoulders, yanking me roughly toward him, his fingernails digging into my skin. I moan in pleasure as his mouth presses more firmly, more confidently, against my neck, locking himself against me and drinking large gulps of my blood. Oh God, it feels so good. So warm. So delicious. Like I always imagined sex would feel like.

"Oh, Jayden," I find myself murmuring as I collapse weakly into his arms. I close my eyes, completely enraptured. The dark, dank alleyway has now become the center of my universe and the rest of my mundane reality is a mere echo of little importance compared to what's going on here. Something to easily give up forever, just for one more moment of this vampiric ecsta—

"Sunny! What are you— Oh, *hell,* no!"

Suddenly, the pleasure is violently ripped away. My eyes flutter open just in time to see Jayden being tossed like a rag doll against the opposite wall—limp and wild-eyed, blood streaming down his chin. Above me stands Magnus, a tall, broad-shouldered shadow holding a large black umbrella over his head to shield the sun. He stares down at me with horrified disbelief on his face and I dimly realize he must have circled back to look for me after I escaped the limo.

I also sense he's so not going to be pleased at catching me with another vamp. Even if my reasons were totally innocent.

"I can explain," I murmur weakly as he scoops me up into his arms.

"I don't think I want to know," he mutters. He starts walking me out of the alleyway and toward the limo, which is idling on the main street.

"Wait! What about Jayden?" I ask, craning my neck to try to look behind me.

"We'll take care of him," Magnus replies in a tight voice. Unfortunately, it sounds more like the mafia brand of "taking care" of someone—cement shoes and the East River—then, you know, making sure all their sweet-sixteen birthday wishes come true.

"Magnus, we have to help him. He's turning into a vampire."

"Yeah," he says grimly. "The whole neck-ripping thing sort of gave that away."

"I know, but . . . I sort of asked him to do that," I protest, suddenly feeling an overwhelming weakness come over me, now that the adrenaline is fading away. My heart thuds sluggishly in my chest. "I thought my Holy Grail–infused blood might help him become mortal again." From behind me, I can see the limo driver dragging Jayden's unconscious body across the pavement.

I wince. Luckily he's a vampire or that kind of treatment would leave some nasty scars.

"Suffice it to say that you thought wrong," Magnus replies as he tosses me into the limo like a sack of potatoes. I wince as my butt hits the seat. Hard. Sometimes vampires forget what it feels like to bruise.

But this is no time to think of myself. "I know, but don't you see? That's my bad, not his. He never would have done it if I hadn't asked him to. If you're going to be mad at anyone, be mad at me."

"That won't be a problem, I assure you."

Argh. He could be so impossible sometimes. And it was tough to fight in my weakened condition. The blackness, now, is fast approaching, but I can't let it claim me until I make sure Jayden has immunity for his crimes. After all, I know the punishment for vampires who take unauthorized drinks from the locals instead of sticking to officially unionized blood donors. And let's just say, it's not just a bite on the wrist.

"Please Magnus, I beg you. Don't let them hurt Jayden. It's my fault he's turning into a vampire and I can't turn my back on him now." My voice breaks at the last part and I look up at him pleadingly.

I catch the flash of indecision in his eyes as he runs a frustrated hand through his hair. I press forward, sensing his weakness. "He saved my life, Magnus. We owe him that."

Magnus sighs, then nods stiffly, turning to the limo driver. "Throw him in the trunk," he instructs. "We'll bring him into the clinic and do some tests before we charge him with anything. See what we're really dealing with here." He turns back to me. "I hope you know what you're asking," he says in a low voice. "My covering up a crime like this could make some vampires question my ability to rightfully lead the Blood Coven. And with all that's been going on, this is not a good time for some power-hungry beta vamp to turn me in to Pyrus and the Consortium. Let's just say our House Speaker isn't too fond of rule-breakers."

"I know, I'm sorry," I say weakly as he crawls in next to me, cradling me gently in his arms. I look up at him with grateful eyes. "But this is the right thing to do, you'll see. Jayden's not some dangerous beast. And if we can help him . . ." I trail off. *Can* we help him? Or is he really doomed to become a creature of the night forever? All because of me.

How will I ever live with that kind of guilt?

Magnus strokes my forehead with a soft hand. "We'll see what the doctors say," he tells me. "And then I'll make a decision. In the meantime, I need you to promise you'll stay away from him."

I frown. "But—"

"I'm serious, Sunny. A new vampire doesn't have complete control of his urges. He could hurt you—even if he doesn't want to." Magnus scowls. "And I'm telling you right now, if I find out he's touched you again—even a mere brush of fingers in a dark hallway, I *will* kill him without a moment's hesitation."

And the black look in his eyes as I fall into unconsciousness confirms that he's not making idle threats.

3

"Sunny!"

I groggily open my eyes, coming face-to-face with my sister, Rayne, who's standing above my bed, peering down at me with a disapproving expression on her heavily made-up face. She's out of her standard-issue vampire rehab pajamas and back in full Goth regalia: black, black, and more black. Making up for lost time, I suppose.

"I can't leave you alone for one second, can I?" she demands.

My hands unconsciously fly to my neck, the memories flooding back to me as I finger the thick white bandage that covers my wound. I appear to be in some sort of white, sterile hospital room that smells a lot like bleach. Magnus must have brought me here after I blacked out in the limo. All around me, machines beep and whir and a catheter attached to my arm drips some kind of unidentified solution into my veins.

I turn my attention back to my sister. "Um, that's rich coming from a girl who spent the last two weeks in the vampire loony bin," I remind her.

"Vampire *rehab*," Rayne corrects as she plops down on the side of my bed. As if that technicality makes it all okay. "Not loony bin. And let me tell you, rehab is *so* hot right now. You should have seen all the vampires going through the twelve steps. I felt kind of bad for some of them. I mean, imagine trying to write down the names of all the people you wronged over a five-hundred-year life span. I'm talking lists longer than the fifth *Harry Potter*. And let's just say it's not always easy to make amends with those you sipped on for supper. Turns out, people tend to hold a grudge about that whole throat-ripping-apart thing. If, you know, they survived the act in the first place."

She shakes her head, remembering. "And then there were the celebs! So many hot vampire celebrities. I wish I could tell you who. But they made me sign this stupid nondisclosure thing saying I couldn't reveal anyone's identity. Though . . . I suppose if you guessed, I might be able to give a nod or something. Or maybe tap my foot . . ."

To be honest, I couldn't care less who was hanging at the Bloody Ford Clinic with my sister. But if it distracted her from asking about how I ended up here in the hospital I was willing to play along.

"Billy Joe from Green Day? That chick from Paramore? R-Patz? Justin Bieber?"

"Um, for the record, Sun, Justin Bieber *sooo* does not make my list of hot celebs. I wouldn't think I'd have to tell you that."

"Spencer Pratt? Eminem? Snooki from *Jersey Shore*?"

"You're not even trying, are you?"

"Well, if it's some weirdo Goth singer from 1980s Germany, I'm giving up now."

Rayne sighs deeply. "Okay, fine. How about charades? Sounds like . . . Ace . . . Rameson."

"Um, have you ever played charades? 'Cause, for one thing, you're not supposed to talk. In fact, it's kind of the only real rule."

"*Ace Rameson*, Sun. Come on!"

I roll my eyes. "Fine, fine. Race Jameson. I get it."

Rayne holds up her hands. "I didn't say a word."

Right. "Okay, fine. I agree. That's pretty interesting," I grudgingly admit. After all, legendary rock star Race Jameson seemed perfectly fine back in October when he helped us with our little cheerleader incident. "I didn't realize he had a blood addiction."

"Well, you know how it is," Rayne says casually. "All those groupies. It must be tough not to take a nibble here and there. And before you know it, you find yourself in the second half hour of your *Behind the Music*." She giggles at her own joke, then turns to me, her expression serious. "Speaking of nibbles. Are we going to talk about your neck now?"

"I think I'd rather talk about the other celebs. Did you happen to see Taylor Momsen? I'm pretty sure she could be a vamp—"

"Come on, Sun. What happened? No one will tell me anything. It wasn't Magnus, was it? 'Cause coven leader or no, I'm pretty sure I could stake his ass if he's suddenly taken to juicing your jugular."

I shake my head, not able to look her in the eye. "It was Jayden," I mutter.

She looks at me sharply. "I'm sorry? For a moment, I thought you said Jayden. But he's—"

"Currently turning into a vampire."

"Well, there goes the neighborhood."

I scowl. I know she's not the hugest Jayden fan—after all, it's in her best interest to keep me with her boyfriend's best friend so we can more easily double-date. But still!

"He saved my life, remember? The night you were too busy playing craps? And while he was so selflessly sacrificing himself for me, he might have gotten infected with the virus." My voice breaks, remembering the frail, pale boy in the alleyway. "If he dies, it'll be my fault."

"Um, he won't die. Vampire, remember? Immortal life, all that jazz? It's sort of the whole point."

"Yeah, I know. But what kind of life . . . ?" I trail off. It's impossible to argue with a girl who, her entire life, wanted nothing more than to be a creature of the night. Even as a kid she refused to eat anything but Count Chocula.

"Jayden didn't ask for this," I try instead. "And also, I think there's something wrong with him. Maybe because he didn't have anyone to guide him through his initial transformation. But he's acting . . . I don't know . . . bizarre."

"Bizarre? Is that what the kids are calling it these days?" Rayne shakes her head in disbelief. "He mistook your neck for a juicy porterhouse, Sunny!"

"Vampires in glass rehabs shouldn't throw stakes," I remind her dryly. After all, she was the one who couldn't control her bloodlust and almost drained Corbin dry back in Ireland. (Which is totally against the Consortium code of conduct, which states vampires can drink only from licensed blood donors.) If Jareth hadn't stepped in and turned poor Corbin into a vampire at the last minute, the Alpha would have ended up a bloodless corpse. Which, in hindsight, wouldn't have necessarily been a bad thing . . .

She snickers. "Well, I'm out of rehab now, baby. And as a slayer, I consider it my sworn duty to stake any vampire who doesn't behave around my baby sister."

Baby. Please. She was born seven minutes earlier than me. And, I might add, has been late to everything ever since. "Even if baby sister gave the vampire in question permission to bite?"

Her wide eyes tell me I've surprised her. Good. "Since when did *you* go all willing-blood-donor chick on me?"

"I'm not. I just thought it might help him." I explain to her my theory on the Holy Grail blood in my veins. "I thought maybe . . . just maybe it would cure him."

"Well, it hasn't," interrupts a male voice.

I look up to see Magnus enter the room. My sister takes one look at the expression on his face and takes off running faster than the Road Runner. Coward!

"Hey, hon," I say casually, trying to will my voice to sound steady and nonchalant. "How's it going?"

He frowns, plopping down in the chair beside my bed. His usually perfectly pressed Armani suit is rumpled and his hair has come loose from its ponytail. "Not great," he replies in a disgruntled voice. "I've missed my flight to Japan and the Consortium has been ringing me off the hook, wondering why I'm not on it."

"Okay . . ." I pause. "And, um, why aren't you, again?"

He gives me a pointed look. "Because a certain girlfriend of mine is in the hospital undergoing a blood transfusion after she decided to offer herself up as a gourmet treat to some hungry stray?"

Oh, right. That.

"Jayden's not a stray," I protest. "He's my friend. And friends help each other. At least, in my world they do."

Magnus reaches over and brushes away a lock of hair that's fallen into my face. He gives me a small smile. "You're very sweet," he says. "Always thinking of others before yourself. Honestly, it's one of the things that made me fall in love with you in the first place."

Hmm. I'm sensing a big "but" coming in for a landing here . . .

"But, Sunny!" Magnus continues, not disappointing me. "You could have very well been killed out there, had I not come along. A new vampire like Jayden doesn't know his own strength. Especially one with no training—he literally wouldn't know how to stop sucking once he started—even if he wanted to. In fact, if I hadn't pulled him off of you, I am quite positive he would have drained every last drop out of your body and still been hungry for more."

I hang my head. When he puts it like that, it does seem like a rather dumb move on my part . . .

"I mean, look at the mess your sister got herself in," Magnus continues. "She sucked the entire mortal life out of Corbin, forcing Jareth to turn him into a vampire. What if I had to do that to you? Would you be okay living the rest of your life as a creature of the night, just to give Jayden his afternoon blood and cookies?"

"I guess not," I mutter, feeling ashamed and stupid. It had seemed like such a good plan at the time . . .

The two of us fall silent, each lost in our own thoughts. Actually, I'm just trying to work up the courage to ask the question I desperately need answered, but at the same time am afraid to know the answer to.

"How is Jayden, anyway?" I blurt out finally.

Magnus looks weary. "He's stable now," he replies. "But I

don't know for how long. I don't know if it's because of the manner in which he was bitten or his hemophiliac blood disorder—but his human cells aren't properly bonding with the vampire ones. Meaning he's not really a vampire. But he's not really human either." Magnus reaches over and takes my hand in his, stroking the back of my palm. "I'm sorry, Sun. I know he's your friend. But I think it might be kinder to just put him down instead of letting him suffer like this."

"Put him down?" My heart reels. I yank my hand away. "Magnus, he's not a dog! You can't just—"

"He's sick, Sun. He can't get proper nutrients from drinking human blood. And so he's literally starving to death, even though we've pumped him with every blood type known to vampire." He shakes his head. "And a sick vampire can be more dangerous than a rabid dog."

I cringe. "But maybe he'll get better! Maybe he just needs more time . . ."

"Normally I'd say yes, but we're in Code Red right now, in case you forgot," Magnus reminds me gently. "The Alphas are readying for battle. And we have no idea what they have in store for us. We need all our top doctors and scientists working on ways to stop them from creating an army of vampiric fairies." He gives me a pitying look. "We just don't have the time or resources to deal with one sick vampire when the whole vampire race is in danger of being obliterated by our enemies."

"But this isn't just any single vampire," I whimper, my voice breaking as I think of my poor, sick friend. "This is Jayden."

Magnus lets out a slow breath as he rises to his feet, his eyes tormented and sad. "Sunny, I know he's special to you. But I don't see any alternative in this case. I wish I did. I really do."

I smile at him, appreciating the effort he's making for my sake. Especially since he's not exactly Jayden's number-one fan. It'd be much easier for him to just let Jayden die—and wipe his only competition off the face of the Earth. But he loves me too much for that. And I love him for loving me that much.

"Master!" A vampire in a white lab coat suddenly bursts into the hospital room, a large clipboard clasped in his hands. He pushes it toward Magnus, pointing down at the charts with a shaky finger. "You said to inform you of any changes. Well, take a look at this."

Magnus studies the chart carefully, his face a mask of solemnity. Then he looks up at the doctor and nods his head. "Thank you," he says. "Keep me posted of any other changes."

The doctor agrees and heads out of the room, clipboard still in hand. I look up at Magnus, who is watching him go, a thoughtful expression on his face.

"What?" I demand, my heart thudding in my chest. "Is this about Jayden?"

Magnus pauses, then nods reluctantly, as if he doesn't really want to tell me the news. As if he has a choice . . .

"Come on, Mag, spill!"

"It would seem . . ." he says slowly. "That your blood actually did do some good for him after all."

My eyes widen. "You mean because of the Holy Grail antibodies in my bloodstream?"

He nods. "While a fully formed vampire would die from receiving a transfusion of Holy Grail–infused blood, since Jayden's still partially mortal, the Grail antibodies actually seem to be helping his human cells fight off the vampire cells. Much like an antibiotic might kill harmful bacteria."

"I knew it!" I cry. "That's awesome news!"

"Don't break out the celebratory champagne just yet," Magnus warns. "He's still got a long fight ahead of him. Vampire cells are extremely strong and he's going to need a lot more antibodies if he has any hope of destroying them altogether."

"Well, I can help. I can give more blood. Whatever he needs!"

My boyfriend shoots me a sharp look. "Believe me, I'm well aware of your willingness to slash open a vein for this guy," he replies. "But it may not be enough to save him. After all, you've only got a trace amount of antibodies in your blood. He'd have to drink gallons for a chance at a real cure. And you just don't have that much to give."

My heart sinks. Was all this hope for nothing then?

"What we need is a very concentrated dose," Magnus muses. "Straight from the source."

The source? "You mean like the actual Grail?" I ask. "Going back to the druids and asking for another drop?"

"Maybe," Magnus hedges. "I just wish this wasn't happening now. The druids are not going to just talk to any vampire who walks up to their door. But I don't know if I can take the time out to go myself." He rakes a hand through his hair. "I've got my duties to the Blood Coven to consider. The Consortium needs me in Japan, like, yesterday."

"Well, the Consortium can hold their vampire horses," I growl, not willing to let this shred of hope be ripped away. "I mean, England's on the way to Japan anyway."

Magnus raises an eyebrow. "Now I know why you're getting a C in geography."

"I meant, if you go around the long way," I correct hastily. "It's just a short side trip. Swing by Glastonbury, grab the Grail blood, cure Jayden, then hop back on the plane to Japan. The most it'll take is a day. And seeing that Japan is a day ahead of us anyway, you'll end up getting there exactly when you're supposed to."

"Your logic never ceases to amaze," Magnus replies dryly. "But yes, I suppose it won't take too much time. And I can work from the plane and keep in touch with phone and e-mail until I'm able to arrive in person."

Yes! "Oh, Magnus, thank you! Thank you, thank you, you thank you!" I cry, throwing my arms around him and squeezing him with all my might. "You won't be sorry. I promise."

"One thing, though, Sunny," Magnus says, pulling away to look me in the eyes. His expression is serious. "You're going to have to come along, too. We may need to give Jayden some small blood transfusions to keep his body fighting until we get the real blood."

I nod eagerly. Happy to be able to help. Happy to not be left at home. Finally, for once in my life, I have an actual purpose. I'm useful to the Blood Coven. Or at least to Jayden.

"Of course I'll do it!" I tell Magnus. "Whatever it takes, I don't care."

My boyfriend gives me a small smile. "You really do care about him, don't you?" he says softly, his voice threaded with envy.

My smile fades as I realize I've inadvertently hurt his feelings with my overt excitement. He knows I still retain a soft spot for the boy who saved my life. A place in my heart where he can never enter.

"I do care about him," I admit, reaching around to pull Magnus close to me. "But not in the way I care about you. My love. My friend." I kiss him softly on the mouth. "And I will never forget this act of kindness you've shown today as long as I shall live."

"And as a fairy princess," Magnus teases, reaching around to stroke my wings through my hospital gown, "that should hopefully be a very, very long time."

4

"The captain has turned off the 'Fasten seat belt' signs," drones a bored-sounding stewardess, "indicating it's now safe to walk around the cabin."

I click out of my seat belt and make my way over to the private plane's bedroom, where Magnus is lounging on his back in the queen-sized bed. (Immortal vampires are always claiming they don't need to buckle up.) He's going over some briefs faxed over by the Consortium, but looks up and smiles as I enter, and pats the side of the bed, inviting me to sit, as he stacks the briefs on a nearby table. I acquiesce, crawling up onto the bed and melting into his waiting arms, resting my head in the crook of his shoulder. He looks down at me and smiles lovingly.

"Hey, baby," he says, moving my hair to the side to better stroke the back of my neck. "How are you feeling?"

"Like a new person," I reply, nuzzling into his chest. "Blood does a body good. Well, a blood transfusion anyway. I'm still not up for making milk shakes out of the stuff or anything."

He chuckles. "Hey, don't knock a double-malt, extra O-negative 'til you've tried one."

I make a face. "Ew.com."

"Well, then can I interest you in a pint of nectar instead?" he asks, stretching out his other arm to open the mini-fridge below the night table. My mouth involuntarily waters as he pulls out a squeeze box of imported fairyland nectar.

"Yes, please," I reply, taking the box from him and stabbing it with a straw. Ever since turning fairy, I've had an insatiable appetite for the stuff. And Magnus, being the best boyfriend in the world that he is, always makes sure to keep a stash on hand.

"How's your work going?" I ask after sipping.

He groans. "I think Pyrus is sending me the worst of it as punishment for not getting to Japan on their timetable."

I shoot him a sympathetic glance. "I'm sorry. I feel bad I've taken you away from your duties."

"It's okay," he says. "He'll live. And, as a bonus, this way I get to spend some extra time with my girl." He takes the juice box from me and sets it on the night table. Then he pulls me back into his arms. "After all, England is a very long plane ride away."

I smile slowly. "However will we pass the time?" I ask impishly as I roll over, pinning him to the bed, looking down at his loving eyes. I lower my lips to his own, tasting his cool, sweet kiss. His hands stroke my back. Lower and lower and . . .

"Have you ever considered joining the mile-high club?" Magnus asks huskily, his fingers skillfully kneading my lower back between my pelvic bones. I swallow hard, feeling the warm tide rise over me, shocked that I'm seriously considering his proposition. Imagine. My first time, with the guy I love, on a luxurious bed, thirty-five thousand miles in the air? What a way to give up the V!

"Mmm," I murmur noncommittally as I attempt to gather my courage. My heart pounds in my chest. Could this really be it? Is the timing finally right? All I'd have to say is one word of assent. One tiny syllable to change my life forever . . . "Oh, Magnus," I whisper. "I'm—"

"ARRGHHHH!"

A piercing cry of anguish interrupts the scene of seduction. Startled, I break from our kiss, sitting up in bed, trying to identify the sound. Magnus grabs my hand and tries to pull me back toward him. "It's just Jayden," he murmurs.

Jayden! God. How can I just be lying here, enjoying all of this, maybe making the most important decision of my life thus far, while he's chained up in the next room, hungry, scared, sick, and alone? Ugh. They should so revoke my friend card.

I squirm out of my boyfriend's grasp. "Maybe I should go check on him," I say, glancing toward the door. "He's probably scared out of his mind."

Magnus frowns. "Francis and Tanner are out there. They'll take care of him."

"But he might be hungry." I glance at my watch. "It's almost time for his feeding."

My boyfriend lets out a long breath. "He'll be *fine*, I assure you. We'll give him some regular blood to hold him over." He tries again to pull me down on the bed. "Just five minutes," he pleads.

I find myself hesitating. Torn.

"It's okay if you don't want to do anything else," he adds, evidently mistaking my guilt for cold feet. "Just cuddle with me. Please?"

Reluctantly, I lie back down on the bed, my body facing the

door. Magnus spoons me against my back, his fingernails lightly scraping up and down my arm. It should feel amazing. But I just can't relax. I keep thinking about Jayden. Hearing his agonizing moans echoing through the cabin.

I sit up in bed. Magnus groans. "*Really*, Sunny?" he asks. "You really want to waste the fleeting time we have together on this guy?"

I turn to him, annoyance welling up inside me. I mean, selfish much? "Magnus, this isn't a vacation, remember?" I retort. "We're only on this flight to begin with to try to save Jayden's life. How can I just lie here and cuddle while he's out there, all alone, scared and suffering and maybe even dying? It just wouldn't be right!"

"What wouldn't be right is for you to go and leave your loving, sweet boyfriend all alone in the bedroom," Magnus replies sulkily. "Refusing to fulfill his lifelong dream of being kissed by his loving girlfriend for five hours straight."

I sigh. There was a time I would have done anything to be kissed for five hours straight by Magnus. But there is no way I could enjoy it now. Not with Jayden in the next room.

I pull out of Magnus's grasp. "I promise, I'll be right back," I assure him as I climb out of bed. "I just want to check on him and maybe give him some blood if he needs it." I turn back to my boyfriend. "Okay?" I plead, hoping for understanding.

But Magnus is already out of bed and walking over to his desk at the far end of the room. "Whatever," he mutters. "I've got that paperwork to do anyway." He sits down at his computer, keeping his back to me.

I sigh. "Please don't be mad."

"I'm not," he replies automatically. "Now if you'll excuse me, I have an important phone call to make." He picks up the plane's phone for emphasis.

Giving up, I head out the door and into the main cabin of the private plane. Francis and Tanner, Magnus's bodyguards, are sitting on the couch, drinking from blood bags and watching *Jersey Shore* reruns, laughing hysterically, while ignoring Jayden's continued moans from the next room.

"Um, hello?" I cry angrily, stepping in front of the flat screen. "What are you doing?"

Francis strains to look around me. "Checking out the Situation?" he quips.

"Well, maybe you should consider the real *situation*," I admonish. "Like the guy you're supposed to be watching? You know, the one crying out in pain and agony in the next room?"

Tanner rolls his eyes. "Newbie vamps are always like that," he rationalizes. "Just like babies, sometimes it's best to let them cry it out."

I squeeze my hands into fists. "Well, I think maybe we should give him some blood."

"He ate two hours ago."

"Well, maybe he needs some more."

"Nobody likes a fat vampire, Sun."

I grit my teeth. "Just give me the damn syringe, okay? I'll feed him myself."

The two meathead vampires exchange glances. "If you move away from the TV . . ."

I take a deliberate step to the side.

"Oh man!" Tanner cries, pointing at the flat screen. "You made us miss the fight scene!"

I glare at him. "If you don't give me the syringe this second, I'll start another one right here in the cabin."

"Fine, fine," Francis says, tossing me the kit. "Go to town." Then he and his buddy turn back to the TV.

Rolling my eyes, I head into the plane's small second bedroom, where Jayden sits on the decidedly less luxurious bed than the one in the master bedroom. His hands and feet are chained to the bedposts and he's staring listlessly at the television, which is, for some reason, tuned in to CSPAN.

Jayden's eyes light up as he sees me. "I think they're hoping I'll stake myself from boredom before we get to England," he says wryly, nodding his head toward the television. I grab the remote and turn the channel to Animal Planet. After all, I know he misses his dog and cat friends back in Vegas.

"Better?" I ask with a small smile as I sit down on the edge of the bed.

He grins. "Much." But from his look, I'm not sure he's referring to the TV.

"Are you okay?" I ask, looking him over. "I heard you moaning in here. Are you in pain?"

"Ugh," he says, looking sheepish. "I didn't realize anyone could hear me. How embarrassing."

"It's okay," I say, resisting the urge to reach out and give him a comforting touch. After all, I promised Magnus I'd stay at arm's length. "Are you hungry?"

"Starving," he admits. "I've drunk tons of blood and it doesn't even begin to satisfy me. The only stuff that does . . ." He trails off, looking longingly at my neck bandage. "And, let's just say, I don't want to be that guy." He bites his lower lip. "God, I'm already humiliated beyond belief that I just drank from you like that. I don't know what I was thinking! I mean, I guess I wasn't thinking at all. I was just so hungry. And once I started—well, I just couldn't stop myself." He trails off, his face red as a tomato. "I'm so sorry, Sunny. If I had hurt you . . ."

"It's okay," I assure him, hating to see him so traumatized.

"I'm totally fine now. And hey, I don't blame you one bit! After all, everyone knows I'm just too, too delicious to resist!"

He grins. "Like a hot fudge sundae with extra, extra whipped cream."

"Really? I was thinking more like a Bloody Mary." I wink.

"Or maybe a bottle of *Sunny* D?"

"Sunny A-negative, to be precise."

We both start giggling hysterically and for a moment everything seems like it's going to be okay. Then reality hits and we both sober.

"I'm so sorry this is happening to you, Jayden," I say, reaching over to squeeze his hand. Yes, I know I'm not supposed to be touching him. But he's chained up. What harm could he do?

He squeezes my hand back with a vampire strength that makes me wince. Oh yeah. That harm. "Sorry," he says quickly, loosening his grip. "I'm just glad you're here now. All of you. I was completely freaking out back in Vegas, on my own, not knowing what was going on or what I could do. But now I feel like I've got this whole vampire family looking out for me. I mean, even if this doesn't work—even if I'm doomed to be a vampire forever—at least I know the Blood Coven's got my back."

I give him a sad smile, my heart wrenching at the hope in his voice. If only he knew the truth. That the Blood Coven isn't the happy family he so desperately wants it to be. That they would have put him to sleep in five seconds flat if it wasn't for my intervention.

But he doesn't need to know that. And once we cure him with blood from the Grail, he'll never have to deal with vampires again. Even if I can never go back to being normal myself, I can make sure that he does. And he deserves that, at the very least.

"I'm going to give you some of my blood," I inform him, rising to my feet and walking to a nearby chair. "If I drain it in here, will that bother you?"

He shakes his head. "No, it's fine," he says. "As long as you talk to me while you're doing it." He pauses, then adds shyly, "I've missed you, you know."

"I've missed you, too," I admit as I sit down on the chair and tie a rubber band around my arm. It makes me feel like one of those heroin addicts you always see in movies. "And I'm really sorry I didn't get in touch once I got back to Vegas. Things have been . . . Well, crazy doesn't even cover the half of it."

"What happened?" Jayden asks. "I thought everything was cool with the Blood Coven and you were just going back to Massachusetts."

I slap at my arm to find a nice vein to draw blood from. "Yeah, so did we. Until our parents dropped the ultimate bombshell on us." I stab at the vein with the hollow needle and a moment later thick, syrupy blood drains down a tube and into the awaiting blood bag. It hurts like a mother, but I remind myself that this small sacrifice may very well save my friend's life and so I'm going to have to deal.

Jayden leans forward in bed, his eyes greedily watching the process. "Bombshell?" he manages to ask without drooling.

And so I give him the 411. About our fae heritage, the threat on our lives, hiding out at Slay School, being kidnapped by fairies. The works. And it's not 'til I come to the part about my dad sacrificing his life to save my sister that my voice cracks and the tears well up in my eyes.

"All this time we thought he was just a selfish jerk," I blurt out, emotions hitting me hard and fast. "Abandoning us to start a new family—not caring whether we lived or died. But instead he was out there that whole time, forcing himself to stay away in an effort to keep us safe from harm. Before he died, he told us that not a day had gone by that he didn't think of us, wishing there was some way to rejoin his family." I make a face. "Meanwhile I was basically sticking pins in a Dad-shaped voodoo doll, cursing his existence on the planet. Some daughter I am."

Jayden gives me a sympathetic look. "You didn't know," he reminds me gently.

I scowl. "I didn't bother to find out either. I just took it all at face value without questioning what was really going on. And now he's gone. And he's never coming back. And I'll never get a chance to tell him how much I love him. How much I've always loved him . . ."

"Maybe you didn't get a chance to tell him," Jayden replies quietly, "but I bet he knows all the same."

I look over at him, through my veil of tears. "I hope you're right."

"I am," he says, his voice leaving no room for argument. "And I can tell you something else, too. Your father would definitely not have wanted you to be sitting here, beating yourself up over the 'what if's.' To negate his sacrifice with regrets. He'd want you to think of all the good times you shared together, don't you think?"

"I suppose so . . ."

"Try it. I mean, what's your favorite memory? Something the two of you shared."

I don't even have to think before answering. "Every night when we were little, he'd curl up in bed with me and Rayne and tell us the best bedtime stories known to man. They'd always start out exactly the same. 'Once upon a time there were two fairy princesses, Sunshine and Rayne.'" I grin. "Who would have thought those stories were actually nonfiction?"

Jayden gives a low whistle. "Fairy princesses. Seriously, that's, like, the sweetest thing ever, Sun!"

"I don't know about that."

"So do you have . . ." Jayden pauses, grinning sheepishly. "This seems so silly to ask."

My face heats as I realize what he's wondering. "What, wings? Yeah. I do."

"Can I see them?" His voice betrays his eagerness, which totally makes me blush hard-core.

"I don't know. They're kind of . . . weird . . ."

"Please? I'll show you my fangs . . ."

"Um, been there, done that, got the T-shirt. Or the bandage, in this case." I remind him teasingly, gesturing to my neck.

"Oh yeah." He grimaces.

The blood bag is full, so I pull out the needle and press a cotton swab over the wound. I'm more than a bit light-headed from so much blood loss and I find I have to grip the chair as I rise to my feet to steady my weakened legs.

Jayden frowns. "I don't like to see you doing this to yourself," he says. "Not for me."

"I want to," I reassure him, sitting back down on the bed and handing him the bag. "And besides, it won't be for long anyway. We'll get the Grail blood and you'll be cured and we'll all live happily ever after."

"Happily ever after. I like the sound of that," he says before sinking his teeth into the bag. I can't help but watch as he sucks the thick red liquid into his mouth, his cheeks flushing with renewed color as my blood drains down his throat. I know I should be creeped out beyond belief, but instead I just feel warm inside, knowing my blood is curbing his desperate hunger and offering him a few moments of peace. The dark shadows in his face seem to fade away and his eyes are brighter and full of life as he drains the bag dry, then sets it down on the nightstand. He looks up at me with an affectionate smile.

"You sure you're a fairy?" he teases softly. "And not an angel, sent from heaven?"

The line should have been cheesy as hell. But with Jayden saying it, it just sounds so sweet. And I find myself blushing all over again.

"Flatterer. You just want another sip," I accuse, trying to keep my tone light.

"No. I just want you."

My heart lurches at the naked truth in his voice.

"Jayden—"

"Sit by me, Sunny," he begs, patting the side of the bed with his bound hand. "Please."

And so I sit. Against my better judgment. Against the voices in my head screaming in protest. I sit beside Jayden and allow him to take my hand in his. He strokes it softly as his eyes find my own, looking up at me with a wide, wondering gaze.

Jayden. Sweet, sweet Jayden.

I start to lean down to him . . .

NO! Common sense returns with a vengeance and I rip my hand away, stumbling backward to put space between myself and the vampire.

"What the hell do you think you're doing?" I demand, staring down at him with horror.

He looks up at me, confused, crestfallen. "What do you mean?"

"You tried to vampire scent me, didn't you? So I'd let you

drink my blood." Suddenly it all makes perfect sense. The sleepy attraction. The almost kiss. Vampire pheromones. Irresistible to mortals. He wanted to lure me into his trap and—

"But I already drank your blood. You gave it to me."

Oh, right. I bite my lower lip. Confused. "Maybe you wanted more?"

"Sunny, I swear I would never—"

I shake my hands in front of my face as I back out of the room. "Whatever. I've got to go. Enjoy *The Dog Whisperer*." And with that, I make my exit, slamming the door behind me, my heart pounding a mile a minute.

"Are you okay?" Francis asks, not looking away from the TV.

I don't answer him. Partly because I don't think he really cares one way or another. But mostly because I'm not sure of the answer myself. *Am* I okay? Did I just fall under a vampire spell?

Or do I still have real feelings for Jayden?

No. That's impossible. I rush past the vampire guards and push into Magnus's bedroom, my whole body shaking as my brain continues to treat me to relentless fantasies of Jayden's lips on mine. I have to break this spell—and fast. And I can think of only one way to do it.

"Sunny! Are you okay?" Magnus rises from his desk, looking concerned. I catch a glimpse in the mirror and realize my face is stark white.

I close the door behind me and lock it.

"I'm fine. Let's do it," I blurt out, desperately trying to catch my breath.

Magnus stares at me. "Do . . . what?"

I grit my teeth. "*It*. You know. Do I have to spell it out?" From his confused face, I gather I do. "You wanted to get your mile-high club membership, remember? Well, let's make it happen."

"But, Sunny, you said . . ."

"I don't care what I said. I want to do it. Now." I start yanking off my shirt.

Magnus is by my side in a flash, so quickly I don't even see the movement. He pulls my shirt back down. "No," he says.

"But I thought you wanted to—"

"I do. Of course I do. But not like this."

I scowl. "Like what?"

"Like you trying to punish yourself for feelings you have for another guy."

I stare at him, horrified. "But I'm not . . ." I trail off, catching his pointed look. "Oh God." I sink down onto the bed. "Magnus, I'm sorry. I just . . . well, I think Jayden just tried to vampire scent me. It was awful. All of a sudden I was thinking all these crazy thoughts and . . ." I realize my boyfriend is shaking his head. "What?"

"He didn't," he says softly.

"Didn't what? Vampire scent me? Yes, he did. He totally did. You weren't there. You don't know how—"

"Sunny, he can't. The doctors . . . well, they essentially neutered him before releasing him into our custody. They removed his pheromone glands so he wouldn't be a danger to mortals while we worked to find his cure."

"Well, they must have missed one," I protest. "Because he totally—"

"Turned you on? He doesn't need a vampire scent for that."

Oh God. I collapse onto the bed, staring up at the ceiling, horrified beyond belief. I can't believe I just told my boyfriend I'm hot for another guy. A guy whose life is dependent on my boyfriend wanting to save him.

Magnus sighs and joins me on the bed. He reaches out and

takes my hand in his. The same hand that, moments before, I let Jayden hold. I feel dirty and gross and undeserving of his caress.

"I'm sorry," I manage to say. "I didn't mean . . ." I trail off. What can I say? What excuse can I give to make any of this okay?

But Magnus places a cool finger to my lips as he continues to stroke my hand. Evidently he doesn't want excuses—or explanations. At least right now. And I am grateful for that kindness.

"Just hold me," he murmurs, curling up in my arms.

And so I do. Forcing myself to stop thinking of Jayden.

5

We land at London's Heathrow Airport the next morning and climb aboard an awaiting limo to continue the two-and-a-half-hour journey to Glastonbury, where the druids commissioned to guard the Holy Grail live. After falling asleep in Magnus's arms on the plane, I'm energized and ready to go. The vampires, on the other hand, are ready for bed—for them, the emerging sun is more powerful than a double dose of Ambien. One by one their heads loll back against the cushy black leather seats as they succumb to a deep vampiric slumber. Even Jayden abandons me for dreamland, though at least he doesn't snore like Francis and Tanner do. I mean, I'd say their snoring would wake the dead, but considering technically everyone in here (except for me) *is* dead (and still sleeping like babies) I guess that's not exactly true.

So I put my earbuds in my ears and turn up my iPod, silently rocking out to a little Lady Gaga as I stare out the tinted window, remembering the last time I journeyed to Glastonbury with Magnus. It's hard to believe it was only last May—it seems a lifetime ago. Back when I thought I was a normal girl living a normal life and my only desire was to get a cute boy to ask me to prom. In just six short months, my simple life has turned upside down and I will never be considered normal again.

Magnus moans softly and cuddles closer to me. I smile down at him. Oh well, normal is kind of overrated anyway.

The last time we arrived in Glastonbury, it was during their annual music festival, and the streets and fields were teeming with raver types. This time, luckily, it's a lot quieter. A charming town with quaint shops and pubs and brick row houses lining the streets. It's a bit of tourist trap—catering to all the King Arthur fans out there—but mostly in a cute, non-tacky kind of way. A far cry from the Vegas strip, in any case.

I get out and do a little exploring while I'm waiting for my team to wake up for the night, buying a few books for Rayne at the independent book publisher Gothic Image on High Street, checking out the castle-like St. Benedict's church, and visiting the famous Chalice Well, which supposedly offers healing waters due to its close proximity to the Holy Grail. (Some people are actually drinking the "healing water," but the fountain looks a little unhygienic to me, so I pass. Besides, I've already gotten healed by the real thing anyway.)

Outside of town you can hike up the Tor, which is this huge hill, topped by St. Michael's Tower. Legend has it this was once an island called Avalon where the druids of Arthurian legend lived. What few people know is underneath this popular tourist destination lies the Holy Grail itself—brought here by Joseph of Arimathea after Jesus died. What we've come all this way to find.

Before I know it, the sun sets and the mist rolls in and the vampires awaken from their slumber as all good mortals head to bed. After receiving Magnus's text, I meet up with the gang at a small, dark pub on Market Street and slide into one of the well-worn wooden booths to discuss our plan. Jayden is no longer chained, but is still flanked by his two vampire jailers, leaving him little chance to succumb to any possible bloodlust.

"The druids are a bit . . . suspicious . . . of strangers, especially vampires," Magnus is explaining. "So I think it's best if just I go alone to their home and you lot wait here."

I frown. "How about I go instead?" I ask. "Seeing as I'm neither stranger nor vampire. In fact, druids and fairies have had a long, intertwined history together." (See? I've been doing my fairy homework!) "Surely they'll be more excited to see me than some undead guy."

"Some undead guy who once gave them a million pounds," Magnus reminds me. "I think they'll remember me . . . favorably . . . despite my fangs."

"Fine. Then let's go together," I determine. "Jayden, are you okay waiting here?"

Jayden nods, though he doesn't look psyched about being left alone with Francis and Tanner, to be honest. Not that I blame him—the two bodyguards are already ordering up pints and tuning in to the local football (soccer) update on the telly. They barely nod good-bye as Magnus and I walk out of the pub and onto the streets. Jayden, on the other hand, doesn't take his sad eyes off of me until we turn the corner out of sight. Which makes me feel more than a little guilty.

"I wonder if it'll be the same guys as last time," I remark, trying to push thoughts of Jayden from my mind as we head down the road. "Or if they totally ditched the whole sacred druid gig once they got ahold of that million you gave them."

Magnus chuckles. "I do wonder how much of that . . . donation . . . ever made it into the goddess's coffers."

"Please. The goddess completely got screwed out of the deal, let me tell you. I'm betting the entire balance went to pints of Stella and front-row seats to the local football matches." I shake my head in disgust. "Druid hooligans."

"Well, I hope you're right," Magnus says. "We need their coffers to be running low to tempt them into considering a second deal."

"Do you think it'll cost another million this time?" I ask. "Or is there some sort of discount for repeat customers?"

"What, like buy one Grail, get one free?" Magnus asks with a laugh.

"Sure. That'd work. At the very least, they should let us put it on plastic so we can score some frequent flyer miles out of the deal."

"Sadly, Sunny, I'm pretty certain the ancient druid sect guarding the Holy Grail does not take American Express."

I huff. "Well, the ancient druid sect needs to get with the new millennium then. Or at least be willing to throw in a set of Ginsu knives with every Holy Grail purchase. I mean, they do know we're in a recession, right?"

Magnus shakes his head, laughing. We turn another corner and I recognize the narrow, cobblestone street the druids call home. Lined with cheerily painted row houses and little curio shops filled with rusty antiques, you'd never know the street was the resting place for one of the most clandestine groups in the world.

Except, you know, for the fact that their front door seems to have been ripped from its hinges and tossed into the street in a pile of shattered glass. Which, let's face it, is not the best way to keep a low profile.

Horrified, I reach down and gingerly pluck the druid's brass knocker from the dirt. The secret symbol of their ancient non–American-Express-taking sect. I hold it up to Magnus questioningly. He takes one look, then dashes toward the house in question, shouting, "Stay here!" as he vanishes through the open doorway.

"Sorry, didn't catch that," I mutter as I rush in after him, down the narrow, gas lamp–lit hallway and into what, at one time, served as a cozy Victorian parlor. Now it's more like something out of a natural disaster flick: furniture overturned, windows shattered, paintings slashed, and ancient-looking books strewn everywhere, their pages ripped to shreds.

"Please tell me this is just the aftereffects of some World Cup party gone wrong," I beg as I survey the scene. But something tells me that even the worst football hooligans wouldn't have made this much of a mess. Not to mention there aren't nearly enough empty beer bottles strewn around to suggest a happy fiesta.

I glance over at Magnus, who appears to be intently sniffing the air like he's Toucan Sam or something. He steps forward, following his nose, over to a swinging wooden door at the far end of the parlor, shoving it open and heading into the next room where, unfortunately, I'm guessing he won't find any Froot Loops. I run after him, pushing through the door and immediately slamming into him on the other side.

"Um, what?" I ask, trying to peer over his shoulder and into the room, which appears to be some sort of kitchen. Though to be honest, I'm not entirely sure I want to know what made him stop short like that. Especially since he currently appears to be shaking in fright. And let's just say vampires don't tend to scare easily.

He takes a step to the side, allowing me an unfortunate up close and personal look at a crumpled body, facedown in a puddle of thick blood. The man is dressed in a druid's robe but his hands and feet have been bound. And while I'm no specialist, I've seen enough *CSI* episodes to conclude that our victim was shot in the back of the head, execution style. Flies buzz cheerfully around the carcass, evidently having a much better night than we are, and it's all I can do not to vomit from the smell of rot permeating the room.

"Come on," I say, grabbing Magnus's arm and trying to drag him back into the parlor. He resists, locking his feet to the floor. Unfortunately even the most self-controlled vampires tend to lose focus when they come across a big pool of free blood just waiting to be drunk. (It's like winning the undead lottery to them.) But I'll tell you right now, if I have to watch my boyfriend mop up this particular puddle with his tongue I will seriously hurl and never be able to kiss him again. Which would suck, big-time, considering what a great kisser he is.

Luckily, a loud moan from the parlor seems to awaken him from his bloodlust. The two of us run back into the main room and look around. Magnus points at a ratty overturned sofa. I grab one end and together we manage to flip it back over to its proper position, revealing another body—this one not so bloody or dead, thank God—curled up in fetal position on the floor.

"Hey, dude! Are you okay?" I ask, toeing the still-living druid with my foot. "What happened here?"

As the man rolls over slowly, his eyes bulge with fright. "Please don't kill me!" he begs, his whole body trembling. "You've already taken everything! I have nothing left to give!"

I squint down at him, taking in the long gray beard and matching robe, tied with a crimson belt. "Llewellyn?" I ask, cocking my head in recognition. "Llewellyn the Pendragon?"

Last time we were here, Llewellyn (probably not his real name) was the one to help us retrieve the Holy Grail blood from under the Tor. Though to be honest, he seemed a lot more majestic and Gandalf the Great–like when he wasn't shaking like a frightened hobbit.

The druid looks up at me in surprise. "How do you know my name?" he demands as he tries to right himself. Magnus grabs his arm and helps him over to the sofa. I notice his robes are bloodstained, but he doesn't appear to be hurt. Unlike his poor friend in the kitchen . . .

"Don't you remember us?" I ask. "We came here last May and donated a bunch of money to your Goddess in exchange for a little Grail blood."

His eyes clear with recognition and he nods his head slowly. "Yes," he says. "Of course. You were the girl who did not want to become a vampire." He glances over at Magnus. "Though you still seem to enjoy keeping their company . . ."

If only he knew. "Yeah, long story, that. But I'm sure it's not half as interesting as what happened here. Why were you hiding under the couch? Who trashed your apartment? And"—I hesitate, not wanting to be the one to break the news if he doesn't already know—"have you seen your friend in the kitchen, by chance?"

Llewellyn draws in a shaky breath. "You mean Collin. Yes. I'm afraid the wheel of life has seen fit to detach my dear friend." He sighs deeply. "I can only hope I shall manage to find him again in our next lifetime."

Ah, right. Being a druid, he'd believe in reincarnation. "I'm sure you will," I try to comfort him. "I'm sure the Goddess will merge your two souls together as one and your destinies will be intertwined for the ages and—"

The druid holds up a hand. "All I'm after is the fifty quid the bastard still owes me. Pretty convenient he goes and gets himself bloody executed before paying me back."

Oh. Right.

"So um, about that," I say, getting back to the subject at hand. "Who did the old executing anyway? I mean, I'm assuming this isn't a normal Friday night in for you guys, right?"

The druid scrubs his face with his hands before speaking. "Early this morning, we gathered before dawn in the parlor to speak our daily prayers and present our offerings to the Goddess mother who made us all," he begins. "But no sooner had we lit our first candle than the front door comes crashing in. A group of five hooded individuals invaded our home, armed to the teeth. Guns, swords, knives—they were a walking, talking armory." He shudders, as if remembering the rampage. "Their leader demanded to know where we kept the Holy Grail."

I swallow hard as Magnus shoots me a worried glance.

"But you didn't tell them, right?" I demand, fear rising to my throat. "I mean, you wouldn't just give it up like that, under threat. That's the whole reason you have this gig to begin with. Your life's mission and all that."

But even as I'm saying the words, I'm remembering the last time we came here. How easily they abandoned their commission for the money we offered in exchange for their secret. And that was without their lives being on the line.

Seriously, the powers-that-be would have been so much better off just leaving the damn thing in a safety deposit box in Topeka.

Sure enough, Llewellyn hangs his head. "We tried," he says

mournfully. "We told them we'd rather die than give up the sacred location of the Grail. And so they started killing us. One by one, execution style, until Collin decided enough was enough. He wasn't prepared to give up his life just for some stupid antique."

"So you gave them the location of the cup," I conclude dully, my heart aching inside of me. Poor Jayden. How am I going to break the news to him that his one shred of hope in regaining his humanity is now likely gone for good?

Llewellyn nods slowly. "I walked one of them to the location myself. A girl—maybe a teenager—it was hard to tell with her red hood shielding her face. In any case, I thought she'd just take a drop or two—all anyone would really need for personal use. But she wanted the whole cup and all it contained. And she had some kind of high-tech laser knife, which she used to chip away the Grail from the stone—stealing it from the sanctuary that's kept it safe for two thousand years." He squeezes his hands into fists. "She sealed the top to prevent any blood from escaping, then ordered me back to the house." His voice cracks. "When we got there, all the other druids—including Collin—were dead."

"But they let you live?" I ask. "I mean, no offense, but why?"

He shrugs. "The girl wasn't happy when she saw all the bodies. She told me to hide under the sofa and play dead. I heard her later in the kitchen admonishing the rest of them for the murders, saying they were unnecessary, seeing as they'd gotten what they'd came for. But the group's leader—who I swear was a vampire—insisted that the Alphas wanted no witnesses."

I shoot Magnus a look, then turn back to Llewellyn. "Wait, what? The Alphas? The Grail robbers said they were Alphas?" It all suddenly starts to make sense. The red robes—that's what the Alphas all wore at Riverdale. After escaping the Blood Coven, Corbin must have rejoined his friends.

"But how would they know to look for the Grail here?" Magnus asks. "Llewellyn's order has been guarding it for two thousand years. There's no way some newbie vampire and his boarding school pals would know of its location."

"Well, *you* knew," Llewellyn reminds him bitterly. "Maybe it's not such a well-kept secret after all."

"Um, it's not like I Google mapped it. I only knew because I once served as a Knight Templar," Magnus replies in a steely tone. "My order was sent to the Crusades to find the cup to begin with. After my maker, Lucifent, turned me into a vampire, I started doing my own research on the side. I traced the cup to your Order in the early 1300s and have been keeping an eye on you ever since." He frowns. "And I certainly never shared the information with anyone."

"Except for her," Llewellyn reminds him, tossing his head in my direction.

Magnus turns to me. "You never told anyone the Grail's location, did you?" he asks. "Think hard."

I bat my eyelashes at him. "Oh, was that supposed to be a secret? Guess I shouldn't have dropped the dime to the Vatican then." Magnus and Llewellyn shoot me looks and I roll my eyes. "I'm kidding. God. Of course I didn't tell anyone."

Okay, fine. I may have mentioned it to Jayden, but he's been under guard the entire time so there's no way he could have spilled. And my sister might know the general vicinity of the Grail, but not the exact address.

"In any case, at this point it doesn't really matter how they learned its location," Magnus interjects. "Only that they have. We have to find them—and the Grail—no matter what it takes. No good could come from the Alphas possessing such a relic."

"Yeah, well you lot have fun with that," Llewellyn mutters,

grabbing a pair of Air Force 1s from under the couch and slipping them on his feet. "I'm bloody done with this gig. I'd rather be stuck pouring pints at a lousy pub for the rest of my days than keep risking my life for a glorified Big Gulp." He yanks off his robes, revealing a vintage Van Halen T-shirt and jeans. "At least now I'll have a decent chance at scoring some health benefits. Damn druids and their 'herbs cure everything so you don't need a doctor' bullshit. I mean, really."

And on that uplifting note, he gives us a little bow, then heads briskly down the hall and out the open doorway, leaving Magnus and me alone in the parlor. My boyfriend watches him go, shaking his head. "Kids today," he snarls. "No respect for holy commissions." Then he turns back to me. "Sorry, babe," he says, giving me a sympathetic look. "I think we're out of luck."

I hang my head. "This sucks. I mean, the Grail's been sitting here for, like, two thousand years and it just happens to get stolen the day before we need it?"

"It does seem a really lousy coincidence. And I don't like the fact that the Alphas have Corbin on the payroll again. They're dangerous enough without actual vampires working for them."

"Well, Corbin didn't want to be a vampire," I remind him. "Maybe he took the Grail so he could turn himself back into a human."

"Maybe," Magnus says, not sounding all that convinced. "Or maybe the Alphas need it to finalize their supernatural DNA cocktail." He scowls. "This could be bad. I have got to notify the Consortium immediately." He rises to his feet and starts out the door.

"Wait," I cry, stumbling after him. "What about Jayden?"

He stops and turns back to me. "I'm sorry, Sunny, I don't know what to tell you. Without the Grail, he really doesn't have much hope."

"Which is why we need to get it back! We should go to Japan!"

"Yes. *I* should go to Japan," Magnus corrects. "You . . . and Jayden . . . can wait for me here if you like."

"Here?" I look around the trash flat.

"I mean at Vampire Manor. You remember the safe house we stayed at the last time you were in England, don't you?"

"Sure, but—"

"I'll have Tanner stay with you as well. He can help you administer doses of your blood to keep Jayden stable while I search for the Grail. And the manor can supply him with doses of their house blood to satisfy his remaining hunger."

I look at him sharply. "What, they just happen to have blood on tap there?"

"It's an all-inclusive," Magnus replies drolly. "Vacationing vampires often desire something a little richer or sweeter than their normally contracted blood donors. Not to mention, have you ever tried to stash a human in your carry-on? Rather impractical to say the least. Not to mention strictly against FAA regulations."

Once again, these vampires have it all down to a science. I guess when you have immortal life, you've got plenty of time to work out all the kinks.

"I don't suppose there's any way for me to convince you to let me come to Japan?" I ask, though I already know his answer before even opening my mouth. "I could look for the Grail myself while you're concentrating on all the other stuff you've got on your plate."

"I'm sorry, Sunny. But the Consortium won't allow it. Besides, to be completely honest, I wouldn't be able to concentrate on my mission if I was always worrying about your safety."

"You wouldn't have to worry. I can take care of myself!"

He gives me a tender smile. "I know you can. I do. But I would worry anyway," he murmurs, reaching over to brush a stray lock of hair from my eyes, then leaning down to kiss me gently on the forehead. His lips are soft, sweet.

Which would be nice if they weren't saying, yet again, *"Sayonara, Sunny."*

6

It's nearly dawn when we reach Vampire Manor and the morning mists are beginning to roll in, making the drive through the wrought-iron gates and down the long, narrow driveway tunneled by overgrown pine trees even more creepy. I try to remind myself that this isn't some kind of haunted house, but rather your local friendly vampire B and B. A resort for fine, fanged individuals to retire at while vacationing in jolly old England. Though don't get me wrong—the place is no five-star resort. No golf course, no swimming pool, and it's a million miles away from any kind of restaurant that might serve pizza. But, as Magnus reminds me, a gloomy English countryside is preferable to creatures of the night, seeing as they can't exactly cruise the Caribbean with their sun allergy.

Not that this makes me feel much better, knowing I'm going to be stuck here, pizzaless, for the foreseeable future. At least I'll have Jayden to keep me company. He's still a little wary from our encounter on the plane, but I can totally apologize for all that once we're alone. At least I know now I'm in no danger of being seduced by him and his non-functioning vampire scent, which means I can just be his friend. Well, in addition to being his breakfast, that is.

As we pull up to the foreboding Victorian mansion, I remember how freaked-out I was the last time we stayed here. Especially once I found out they'd arranged for Magnus and me to share a bed, assuming we were actual blood mates. After all, back then I barely knew the guy. And I certainly didn't trust some bloodsucker to do the right thing.

Who knew in less than a year he'd become my best friend and true love? The one person in the world I'd want to curl up with in a big smooshy canopy bed for two, pulling the curtains closed to block out the sun and sleeping for at least a week.

But, of course, now the bloodsucker in question has other plans.

"You'll be safe here," he tells me as the chauffer comes around and opens the door. Jayden and his guards scramble out, but Magnus grabs onto my hand, evidently not ready to exit just yet. "Safer than you would have been in Vegas, even. This place is known only to vampires and is extremely protected with the latest in high-tech security. The Alphas wouldn't stand a chance infiltrating it—even if they did know of its location, which, I can assure you, they do not."

"What about Rayne?" I ask, suddenly remembering my sister is now out of rehab. Could she be in danger, remaining in Vegas? "Maybe you could arrange for her to come here and meet us? You know, if it's all safer and stuff." Plus, even though she can be annoying at times, at the end of the day, she's pretty entertaining. And from what I remember about the cobwebby interior of this place, I'll need quite a bit of entertainment to keep my sanity in the coming weeks.

Magnus groans. "Your *sister*," he says, ". . . well, let's just say, true to form, she exhibited some . . . behavior unbecoming to a vampire . . . last time she was across the pond. The English Rose Coven has made it very clear she is not welcomed anywhere near their jurisdiction."

Of course. Leave it to Rayne to piss off the welcoming committee. "But that was before she went to rehab," I remind him. "The girl's reformed. A new vampire. I'm sure she'd behave herself if they let her back in." Well, okay, technically I'm not 100 percent sure of this. After all, if you look up "loose cannon" in the urban dictionary, I'm pretty sure you'd find her picture. But I'd be here to keep her line. And if it would keep her out of danger . . .

"Actually . . ." Magnus purses his lips, looking pained.

"What?"

"It's been decided . . . against my better judgment, of course . . ."

Sudden realization hits me hard. "You're taking her to Japan," I finish dully. Of course they are. Once again my sister gets to be in the midst of all the action while I'm left behind to be babysat by Vampire Poppins. It's so not fair.

"Like I said, it wasn't my decision," Magnus restates. "But your sister is the only known vampiric fae in existence today. We may have need of her." He pauses, then adds, "Anyway, I thought you'd prefer to stay with Jayden."

"Jayden could come to Japan," I reply automatically. "This

way if we find the Grail, he can just drink the blood right away, instead of you having to FedEx it back across the world. 'Cause imagine if it got lost in the mail! That would be—"

"Sunny, look at him," Magnus interrupts, pointing to my friend, who's currently leaning up against the limo. "Does he look in any shape to travel to the front lines of a supernatural war?"

I reluctantly look over, realizing he's right. Jayden looks frail and sick, with hollow eyes and trembling hands. He needs to stay somewhere safe and comfortable if he has any chance of surviving all of this. And I need to stay with him to keep supplying him with my blood. Which offers Magnus the perfect excuse to keep me here and out of harm's way.

"Don't think I don't see what you're doing," I growl. "But fine. I guess I've got no choice. I'll stay with Jayden and give him his transfusions. But you'd better stay on the ball out there in Japan," I add. "Don't get so caught up in the war that you forget about me and the Grail."

Magnus sighs, suddenly looking weary. "When are you going to learn to trust me, Sunny?"

"I do trust you. It's just—"

He gives me a pointed look.

"Look, I know you love me," I try to explain. "But I also know how loyal you are to the Blood Coven. And I'm totally cool with that, really. I want you to be able to protect your people and all. But sometimes—I wonder. If push came to shove . . ."

"Yes . . . ?" He's going to force me to spit it out.

"Would you pick me over the Consortium? If Pyrus handed you a direct order, I mean."

He groans. "Why do you do this to me, Sunny?"

"That's not exactly an answer."

His eyes narrow. "What do you want me to say? That I'd

choose you? No matter what? That's a little immature, don't you think?"

I can feel my hackles rise. "Well, no offense, dude, but let's just say you don't exactly have the best track record. In fact, you outright dismissed me when I tried to warn you about Jane back in Vegas. Hell, you were too busy being the Consortium's lap dog to even consider the fact that I might be on to something. So, sorry for wanting a little reassurance this time around."

"Yes, I was wrong. You were right. And I apologized for that. Many times, in fact. And you *said* you forgave me," he reminds me bitterly. "Which, from what I understand about forgiveness, means you're no longer able to hold the incident over my head every time you don't get your own way."

"My own way?" I repeat, fury burning inside me now. "You think that's what this is about? You think I want to be stuck here, in some creepy vampire holiday house, draining my blood daily to help a sick vampire, all the while wondering if my boyfriend is dead or alive? Please. I'd much rather be back in Vegas, playing field hockey with my new friends, enjoying a normal, everyday life. But I've put normalcy on hold. All because of you. Which is fine—I'm totally cool with doing that. But I want the same in return."

"Oh, right. Because my life is *never* disrupted because of you," Magnus retorts sarcastically. "Let me tell you, I had a jolly Carnival Cruise holiday scouring the globe after I found out you'd been kidnapped by fairies. Oh and filing that report to the coven, letting them know I was keeping a sick, unlicensed, possibly dangerous vampire alive because my girlfriend had feelings for him? That was a bloody picnic, let me tell you. Not to mention getting written up by Pyrus for disobeying their orders to head directly to Japan . . ." He yanks at his ponytail, freeing his hair. "Yes, you've got it all figured out, Sunny. I'm a bloody selfish bastard and Pyrus's flunky and you're always getting screwed."

The raw anger in his voice cuts me like a knife—and his words are salt in the wound. I cringe. What was I thinking—challenging his loyalty? Sure, he's made mistakes. But it's not like I haven't, too.

"Look, Magnus, I—"

He waves me off. "Sunny, I promise I will do everything in my power to find the Grail and save Jayden's life. But please—try to see the bigger picture here. You want to save one vampire. I'm trying to save the entire vampire race. Don't put me in the position where I have to choose between the two."

"I know, I know!" I cry, guilt wracking my insides. "I'm sorry. I know you're dealing with a lot. And I do trust you. I swear."

But my boyfriend just looks at me with sad eyes. "I don't think you do," he says softly. "You want to, but you can't. You say you've forgiven me. But you still resent me, deep inside. And that's a problem."

I feel the tears welling in my eyes. "But I—"

He shakes his head. "We're going to talk about this when I return, okay?" he says. "Because if you really can't trust me. . . If you truly believe I don't have your best interests at heart . . ." He swallows hard. "Well, I don't know if any of this is going to work."

I look up at him, horrified beyond belief. Did he just imply what I think he did? Oh God, I didn't mean . . . My heart starts slamming in my chest. "Magnus—"

But my words are cut off as the chauffeur rolls down the back window. "Sorry to interrupt, m'lord," he says. "Your plane is scheduled to leave within the hour."

"Right." Magnus purses his lips and then turns to me. "I need to give Tanner some instructions. I suggest you go in and find your accommodations. I'll be in touch as soon as I can."

His cold voice makes me shiver. I want to say a million things—to apologize a million times—but I know it's not the time or place and I don't want to make things more difficult than I've already made them. "Okay," I croak. "Can I just get a—"

But he's already out of the limo before I can finish my request for a hug good-bye. Maybe it's for the best. I'm not sure, if I had him in my arms right now, whether I'd be strong enough to let him go.

So instead I reluctantly step out of the limo and into the chilly, predawn air. Jayden bounds over to me, his face still pale, but his eyes alight with excitement. "Sunny, have you seen this place?" he asks, his voice full of wonder. "It's amazing. Like something out of a fairy tale. I've never seen anything like it. I wonder when it was built. I mean, we don't have anything this old in Vegas."

"Please. Even *I'm* older than Las Vegas," scoffs an approaching female voice.

I look up, my eyes widening as three vampire-supermodel types strut out the front door and down the steps, regarding Jayden with hungry eyes. They stop in front of him, fanning out in a semicircle. There's a blonde, a redhead, and a brunette. All beautiful. All appearing to be about seventeen. But probably more like seventeen hundred.

"Who are you, handsome?" queries the redhead in a Northern English accent. Her otherworldly blue eyes give Jayden a slow, sultry once-over. As if he's a steak dinner she'd love to devour. "And what brings you to Vampire Manor?"

7

Jayden takes a hesitant step back as the three vampire girls circle him like hungry hyenas.

"Um, I'm Jayden," he stammers. "I'm, um, new."

The girls exchange amused glances and giggle. "Fresh blood," coos the brunette. "How lovely."

Jayden throws a worried look in my direction and I try to break in to save him, but the girls manage to complete their circle, locking their arms around my friend and effectively shutting me out.

"I'm Elizabeth," introduces the redhead. "And this here is Katie and Susan." The other two girls bob in refined greeting. They look like Serena and Blair from *Gossip Girl*, but their mannerisms scream Victorian England. So I'm placing them at about 160 years old, give or take.

"We're from the Lakes District up north," explains Katie.

"Lakes District?" Jayden repeats, staring at her, as if mesmerized. I frown. Could vampires use their vampire scents on other vampires? 'Cause I gotta admit, he looks completely smitten by all three of them right about now. A look, I might add, he usually reserves for me.

Not that I'm jealous or anything. I just don't think it's a great idea for a sick vampire like Jayden to be looking to hook up right now. He's got bigger things to worry about—like concentrating on his recovery. Not to mention keeping me company in this godforsaken place until Magnus comes back.

"Have you never been to the Lakes District? It's a beautiful place, but dreadfully dull in the winter," Susan explains. "So we come down here for an extended holiday from time to time."

"Our dear Maker, Professor Lucedio, is the kindest vampire you'll ever meet in your life," adds Elizabeth. "He lets us stay anytime, free of charge." She turns to her friends. "And how lucky it is, girls, that we chose this weekend to come! Otherwise we might have missed our chance to meet Mr. Jayden altogether." The other two nod in excited agreement. I resist the urge to roll my eyes.

"Well, it's very nice to meet you," Jayden replies politely, reaching out to shake all of their hands. This makes them giggle all over again. Not to mention bat their eyelashes and swish their hair. And here I thought vampires could afford to be a bit more subtle.

"What coven are you from?" Elizabeth purrs, sidling closer.

"Oh!" Jayden looks slightly taken aback by the question. "Well, I'm not from any coven, I guess," he stammers. "But Lord Magnus, from the Blood Coven, has been nice enough to take me under his wing until we've figured things out."

I scowl. *Magnus* was nice enough? Magnus wanted to put

him down like a dog. *I* was the one who fought to get him here. Risked my relationship to try to save his life. But hey, name-drop my boyfriend all you want, I guess, if you think it'll impress the ladies. Forget all about poor old Sunny, who saved your life.

"Oh, Magnus!" the three girls squeal in unison. "We *love* Lord Magnus."

"He's so handsome!"

"And so debonair."

"A former knight in shining armor—it doesn't get more romantic than that."

"Not to mention he's—"

"—MY boyfriend," I cut in curtly, pushing my way into the circle. The girls' excited faces twist into scowls.

"And *who* might you be?" sniffs Elizabeth.

"Oh, sorry!" Jayden looks at me sheepishly, as if he'd forgotten I'd been standing behind him the whole time. Maybe he had. "Um, girls, this is my good friend Sunny."

The three she-vampires attempt to stare me down with narrow, suspicious eyes. "You look . . . familiar," Susan states. "Why is that?"

"Wait—isn't she that vampire slayer we kicked out of the coven?" Katie asks. "You remember, that bitch who pulled out her stake after we tried to offer her some very expensive blood?"

"Yes, that's definitely her." The girls surround me menacingly, baring their fangs. "How dare you show your face here?"

I hold up my hands in protest, suddenly remembering the story my sister told me of her last trip to England. "Hold it. You can stop the lynch mob right there! That wasn't me. That was my sister, Rayne. We're twins. Well, on the outside anyway. I swear to you I have much better manners than her. Not to mention I'm not a slayer."

Susan purses her lips. "You're not a vampire either."

"Sunny's a fairy!" Jayden chimes in, oh so helpfully.

Great. Here we go.

The girls' eyes widen with interest. Susan grabs my arm and starts sniffing me. Ew. I take a hasty step backward, ripping my arm from her grasp. "Do you mind?"

"Yup. I thought I smelled something," Susan affirms, wrinkling her annoyingly perky little nose. "Pixie sweat. Smells just like rotten nectar."

Ooh, that does it. "Look, I'm no freaking pixie, okay?" I say, lifting my chin haughtily. "I'm Princess Sunshine of the Sidhe Light Court. My mother is queen and I'm next in line for the throne, if you must know."

Take that, vampire commoners. I pause, waiting for the respectful looks such a claim should entitle me to. But instead, the stupid girls burst into laughter. Hmm. So not the reaction I'd been hoping for.

"Well, la-di-da, ladies!" cries Elizabeth. "Who knew little old us would be blessed by a visit from actual royalty."

"Perhaps we should be bowing down to Her Majesty," adds Susan. "Paying our respects."

I can feel my face flame. Why did I have to go and say that? Stupid, Sunny. Way to try to fit in.

"Look, I'm not here on any fairy business," I attempt. "I'm just acting as Jayden's donor, that's all. But I expect a little . . ." I trail off, catching their faces, which are currently twisted in sudden disgust. "What?"

"Ew," Katie cries. "Are you serious?"

"You drink fairy blood?" Elizabeth asks, turning to Jayden. "Isn't it completely gross?"

"I tried deep-fried fairy blood at the Vampire World Fair a

few years ago. It's so disgustingly sweet," adds Susan. "Not to mention completely fattening, what with all the nectar and crap you lot consume."

"A friend of mine knows someone who knows someone who got addicted to the stuff. He grew to, like, three hundred pounds before he spontaneously combusted one day."

"Don't worry, Jayden," Elizabeth says, placing a comforting hand on my friend's shoulder. "We brought some great vintages from our blood cellar up north that we'd love to introduce you to."

"Wait 'til you taste a 1547 Henry the Eighth," adds Susan. "You'll never want to go back to that glorified pixie ripple again."

"Look," I interject. "I'll have you know that my blood is the only thing that—"

But a dark shadow looming behind the girls makes me clamp my mouth shut. I gulp. It's Dracula. Or, more precisely, the manor's proprietor, Professor Lucedio, who just happens to look exactly like the legendary count of old, complete with tuxedo and black cape. I remember meeting him the last time I was here and he doesn't look any less scary, even though Magnus assures me he's actually quite a marshmallow on the inside.

"Ladies, what is going on here?" he demands. "Don't you have anything better to do than bother my guests?"

The girls look at one another and titter. Then they look back up at their Maker with wide, overly innocent eyes. "Why, no, Professor," says Elizabeth. "We have nothing better to do at all."

"Unless someone were to let us borrow their sweet little Mini Cooper . . ." Susan adds.

The professor sighs and fishes out a set of keys from his cape's inner pocket and hands them to the girl.

"And your credit card?" Katie chimes in. No wonder they like coming to visit this guy. "You know, in case we need . . . gas?"

"Progeny," he mutters, rolling his eyes as he reaches for his wallet. He hands a black American Express card to Katie. "I'd better not see any charges from the Manolo Blahnik store this time," he scolds.

"No, Professor," the girls chime in unison. Though under Elizabeth's breath I can swear I hear, "I prefer Jimmy Choo anyway."

"Jayden, you want to come with us?" asks Susan. The three girls look at him hopefully.

He glances at me, then at the girls. "Um . . ."

"Now, girls, why don't you let our guest get himself settled in before you try to abscond with him," Professor Lucedio suggests, his voice leaving no room for argument. "He must be tired from his journey." He shoots Jayden a meaningful look, and thankfully my friend nods in agreement.

"Oh, fine," Elizabeth grumps. Then she winks at Jayden. "We'll see you later!" she says saucily before she and her friends skip over to the detached five-car garage at the far end of the driveway and pull open one of its doors.

"Be back before sunrise!" Professor Lucedio calls after to them. Then he turns back to us, shaking his head. "Sorry about that," he says. "They mean well. But they can be a bit much at times."

"That's one word for it," I say, watching them peel out of the driveway at a thousand miles an hour. I hope their holiday is over soon and they pack up and head back to the Northern wastelands ASAP. 'Cause bunking with these bitches is so not going to be any fun.

I notice Jayden watching them go, a wistful expression on his face. Traitor.

A motor's roar behind me brings my attention back to the present. I turn, just in time to see our stretch limo pull away from the curb.

"Magnus!" I cry, dashing after it. I can't believe he just took off like that, without even saying good-bye. He must be more pissed than I thought. My heart pounds in my chest as I run after the vehicle, my lungs seizing with exhaust. But it doesn't slow down, and soon I'm forced to stop, leaning over with my hands on my knees, trying to clear my throat. I feel a hand on my shoulder and whirl around, expecting it to be Jayden, come to comfort me. Instead, it's the professor, looking down at me with a concerned expression.

"He'll be fine," he assures me, mistaking my heartbreak for worry. "He's tough, that one. We fought side by side during the Werewolf Uprising of 1863. They called him the Biteproof Baron. Nothing could stop him from storming the wolves' lairs and rescuing the humans they'd trapped within."

I reluctantly allow the professor to lead me back to the house as I try to digest this new piece of Magnus's history that I knew nothing about. It should make me feel proud inside—my boyfriend, defender of the helpless. But instead it just reminds me of how much I don't know about him. Not to mention how many lifetimes he's lived without needing me by his side. I'm just a ripple in his endless pond of existence. And if he grows displeased with me, I'm sure he'll have no problem moving on, taking my crushed and broken heart along with him as he goes.

"Are you crying?" Jayden asks as we approach.

"No!" I retort, angrily swiping my eyes with my sleeve. "I've got allergies, okay?"

"Oh. Right. Sorry." He hangs his head and stares down at the ground, which only serves to make me more miserable. What am

I doing, resenting him for talking to girls? He has every right to make friends. Or girlfriends. I had my chance to be with him. I chose Magnus instead. And now I need to learn to live with my decision and let him move on.

But as I catch a glistening tear caught in his black, sooty lashes, I realize that's going to be easier said than done.

"Please, follow me inside," Professor Lucedio instructs, clapping his hands in stiff-upper-lip fashion. "Rufus will bring your things to your rooms." He starts up the imposing set of stone front steps, flanked by two gargoyles.

I give one last look down the now empty driveway, then reluctantly trudge up the steps, my legs feeling as if they're made of lead. I still can't believe Magnus didn't even say good-bye . . .

8

About twenty minutes later, I find myself lying on a king-sized bed in a small bedroom, very similar to the one Magnus and I shared on our first trip here so long ago. (Okay, it was technically just last May, but with all that's happened this year, it feels like a lifetime ago.) At the time I didn't want to touch him—and he'd gallantly offered to sleep on the floor so as not to offend me. But instead, I let him stay, and while we both fell asleep apart, somehow, through the night, we unconsciously came together. I didn't want to admit it at the time, but I was already falling fast for him.

What I wouldn't give for another night like that now. Curled up against him, his strong arms wrapped around me, refusing to let go as we drift off to dreamland together without a care in the world. Instead I'm cold and alone and scared and he's boarding a plane to go halfway around the world. And he didn't even say good-bye.

I toss and turn in my bed. Will Magnus really keep his promise and make seeking out Jayden's one hope a top priority? Or will he get caught up in Consortium business the moment he steps off the plane and, despite his best intentions, allow the quest for the Holy Grail to fall by the wayside? How long will I be stuck here, waiting, wondering? And why can't I just trust him to do the right thing?

Is it because of what he did in Vegas? Or something deeper than that? Are my past experiences with my dad and all his broken promises still tainting my ability to believe my boyfriend? Even though my father's actions were all justified in the end and it turned out he wasn't the terrible father we thought he was, it's still hard to reconcile the feelings of abandonment I experienced through his extended absence. And that makes it nearly impossible to truly believe that there's really someone out there now who loves me enough to never let me down.

And thus I force Magnus, time and time again, to pay for all my emotional baggage. Which is so not fair to him. If we want this to work—and oh God, I do, I do—I need to work on my own issues as much as he needs to work on his. One way or another, I need to learn to trust him. With all my heart, soul, and mind. Otherwise, like he said, why are we even bothering?

Realizing I'll never be able to sleep, I slide out of bed and start unpacking. The lights are dim—probably to accommodate the manor's normally nocturnal guests—so I draw back the curtains, hoping for some kind of early-morning light. But outside, the darkness still looms and rain sluices down, thunder cracking and lightning slashing through the sky. I shiver, then force myself to turn back to the chest of drawers.

I'm almost fully unpacked when I hear a firm rapping on the door. "Come in," I say, pushing the last drawer closed and straightening up. I catch my reflection in the mirror and try to pat down my messy hair to better greet my visitor. But the hollows in my eyes from lack of sleep aren't so easy to fix.

The door pulls open and Rufus, the human butler, steps in, carrying a syringe. "Sorry to disturb you," he says in a stiff English accent. "But I've been instructed to prepare for Master Jayden's feeding."

Of course. I nod and sit down on the bed, holding out my arm to him to let him do his thing. By this point the needle no longer even hurts that much and soon I'm watching the blood drain from my veins, down a tube and into a blood bag.

"So how is Jayden doing?" I ask. "Can I go see him?"

"He's fine," Rufus replies. "The girls are back and keeping him entertained."

Of course they are. "Well, I'd like to see him. Can you show me where he is after we're finished?"

Rufus shoots me a sympathetic look. "I'm afraid that's not possible."

"Excuse me?"

"Professor Lucedio gave me explicit instructions. You're to stay in your room until the sun rises."

"He did?" A cold feeling starts creeping over me. "But why?"

"This is a hotel for vampires," Rufus reminds me curtly. "And not all of our guests are . . . accustomed to sharing such close quarters with mortals."

"*You're* mortal."

"Yes. And I've had some . . . accidents . . . in the past because of it." He tilts his head to the side and I gasp to see a myriad of white scars crisscrossing his neck. Ouch.

"Dude. I hope you got major workers' comp for that."

He chuckles softly. "I'm used to it by now," he says. "And guests are usually respectful enough just to take a sip or two."

"Is that even legal? I thought it was forbidden to take from anyone who's not a sanctioned donor."

Rufus shrugs. "Sometimes, when you're on holiday, you're tempted to . . . let your fangs down, so to speak. And we, as a premiere holiday destination, find we're better off looking the other way when it comes to that sort of thing. After all, there's no use risking our impeccable TripAdvisor rating just over some random inconsequential indiscretion."

"No offense, but that seems a bit more than an indiscretion . . ."

"Which is why we need to keep you here," Rufus concludes. "Especially since you're not only mortal, like me, but you've got fey blood in your veins as well—which can be very addicting to some vampires. And let's just say you don't want to put temptation directly in their paths. You may not live long enough to regret it." He pulls the needle from my arm and presses a cotton swab to the wound. "It's better that you just stay here and rest, trust me."

I sigh. So basically what he's saying is I'm stuck under house arrest for my own safety for the foreseeable future. Stupid weak-willed vampires, unable to control their own bloodlust.

"And when morning comes and all good vampires are resting in their coffins or beds, you can come downstairs," he adds. "I'll cook you a big delicious breakfast, then give you a tour of the entire place."

"Great." I feel bad—I know he's trying to be nice and accommodating. But what good will walking around in the daytime do me? Jayden will be asleep with the rest of them by then. So much for him keeping me company. I am seriously going to die of boredom in this place, aren't I?

"Look, I totally get it," I say. "But maybe you could send Jayden up to my room if I can't go down to see him? I want to make sure he's okay, at the very least."

Rufus gives me another pitying look. "Lord Magnus gave explicit instructions you're not to be alone with the boy during your stay here."

I frown. *Why, Magnus? Because he lusts for my blood? Or because I might be lusting for something else . . . ?*

Rufus pats my shoulder comfortingly. "Don't worry, miss. As I told you, the girls are seeing to his every need. He is having a grand old time down there with them in the library. His laughter rings through the halls."

Awesome. Just . . . awesome.

The butler rises from the bed and collects his things, then heads to the door. "Please feel free to use the intercom if there's anything you desire," he says, pointing to a little box on the wall. "Your door is programmed to unlock at sunrise."

And with that, he exits the bedroom, closing the door firmly behind him. A moment later I hear an electronic click, dooming me to my fate. Because I'm a masochist, I run to the door anyway, trying to force it open. But, of course, it doesn't budge.

I slide down the wall and onto the floor, hugging my knees to my chest, mixed emotions swirling inside of me. Did Magnus know this was what it'd be like here? That I'd basically be a glorified prisoner during my stay? And if so, he was okay with all that?

And while I'm stuck in vampire jail, Jayden's living it up with those ditzy girls, all wanting to jump his bones. Probably completely forgetting that I even exist.

Seriously, boys can completely suck sometimes.

9

In the movies, we often see our heroine get trapped by the bad guys and though there's a completely obvious, easy way for her to escape, she doesn't notice it until moviegoers are literally screaming at her at the top of their lungs to stop being too stupid to live and just go through the freaking window already.

But, let me tell you, when you're in the same situation yourself, it suddenly doesn't feel all that black and white. You're scared, you're stressing out, and your thought processes aren't being lubricated by buttery popcorn and a giant diet Coke.

So yeah, it takes me about fifteen minutes and a rousing mind game of "What Would Rayne Do?" to realize that though Rufus locked the door, the large window looking down onto the grounds remains fair game. Especially for a fairy with wings.

Of course first I have to break said window, which, I might add, looks a lot easier in the movies than in real life. In fact, it takes about thirteen exhausting attempts and the assistance of a nearby armchair to finally shatter the glass enough so I can crawl through and climb onto the ledge without cutting myself on the nasty shards jutting out from the frame.

Once outside, I press my back against the wall of the mansion, praying my feet won't slip out from under me as they seek solid purchase on the ledge, slick from the downpour of rain. My vision reels as I dare look down to the ground, four stories below, and my stomach roils in protest. Suddenly this doesn't seem like the most genius plan ever after all.

To be honest, up until this point I've never trusted my wings to take me anywhere I couldn't already jump and live to tell the tale. Rayne once dared me to fly off the Stratosphere Hotel in Las Vegas but I wasn't having any of that, let me tell you. Heights are so not my thing.

Lightning slashes through the sky, followed by thunder that seems to shake the whole manor house. More than half of me wants to just climb back inside—to wait until morning and figure out a less death-defying escape plan.

But then I see my sister's disappointed face. And I hear Magnus telling me I need to stay home where it's safe. No one believes I can be the kick-ass twin. I need to prove them wrong. And what better opportunity to do so than to jump off a four-story window ledge in the pouring rain?

Sucking in a breath and closing my eyes, I unfurl my wings and . . .

Okay, I know you're expecting me to say "jump," but to be honest, that might be overstating my next move a bit. Fine, I'll admit it. I fell. But you try reaching behind your back to pull your wings out from under your shirt on a ledge that's about three inches wide without having your foot slip.

And so I fall, careening toward the ground, wings still trying desperately to unfurl. I'm like a paratrooper whose chute didn't open and I'm quite positive I'm soon to become intimately acquainted with the ground below.

Oh God, I should have stayed in my room! Accepted my non-kick-ass twin status and— A gust of wind catches my wings, launching me upward again like the second part of the *Twilight Zone* Tower of Terror ride at Disney World. I suck in a breath, readying myself for another tumble, but luckily life isn't like a Disney ride and instead of a second drop, the wind guides me gently to the ground again. I won't claim my landing was a perfect ten, by any means, but I don't seem to have any broken bones, so that's something at least.

I let out a long breath, trying to still my wildly beating heart, rejoicing in the feel of solid ground beneath my feet. Seriously, if I ever manage to get out of all this alive, I'm so going to take flying lessons over the summer when I'm visiting Mom in Fairyland.

Gathering my courage, I start traversing the perimeter of the old Victorian mansion as rain sluices down, soaking me to the skin. I shiver as I slip around a corner, praying to find an open door so I can grab Jayden and the two of us can make our escape.

Instead, just my luck, I come face-to-face with a nasty-looking guard dog.

I back up slowly, holding my hands out in front of me. "Good boy," I try, my voice hoarse and barely audible over the wind and rain. "Sit. Stay. Um, roll over?"

But the dog evidently doesn't have a solid grasp on the English language or just prefers to do his own thing and, instead of obeying my simple commands, steps forward, baring his teeth, a low growl emitting from his throat.

Yikes. My eyes dart around, desperate for an escape route. I know at any moment he'll lunge at me full force and my daring, amazing, cool-as-hell escape will mean nothing as I literally become dog meat.

"Good boy," I try again. "Um, fetch?" I grab a nearby stick and throw it off to the side. But the rabid-looking dog doesn't even glance in its direction. Great.

Out of the corner of my eye, I notice a cracked window leading into the mansion. I might be able to jimmy it open, but will I have time to do so before the dog makes me his midnight snack? Normally I'd just use my wings again—fly above the bite range—but the rain has soaked them through and they're so heavy I can't even lift them, never mind fly.

So instead I slowly move toward the window, trying not to make any sudden moves. The dog watches with narrowed, blood-shot eyes, his tail swishing suspiciously from side to side. I lock my fingers underneath the weather-beaten window frame and pull upward, praying it'll slide open easily and allow me an escape route.

Of course, it seems to be stuck fast. This is not my lucky day.

But I grit my teeth, not willing to give up. I apply added pressure, though still slowly, as to not freak out the dog. "Good boy," I mutter, using my entire body weight against the window. *Please open, please open.* "Good, good boy."

At last the window frame lets out a loud groan and gives in. Which should be a relief, except for the fact that, let's just say, the high-pitched creaking sound it makes as it slides upward is not exactly music to the dog's ears. Instead it's the excuse he's been waiting for. He snaps his teeth and makes his move, lunging at me with full force.

I don't hesitate, throwing myself through the window. But I'm not quick enough and the dog's jaws wrap around my ankle. I yelp in pain as sharp teeth dig into my skin, and I flail half in and half out of the house. I try to kick at the dog with my other foot, forcing him to let go. (Yes, I know, kicking dog = completely un-heroic but tell me you'd do differently if you had Cujo's rabid mouth locked down on one of your appendages.)

My foot finally connects with the dog's head and he yelps in pain, loosening his grip on me. I use the momentary lapse to my advantage and squirm the rest of the way through the window, turning around and slamming it shut behind me.

I collapse on the floor, my breath coming in short gasps. That was too close. My ankle throbs, deep puncture marks in the flesh, and I pray the dog wasn't actually rabid. I rip my shirt, binding the wound with the cloth. At least the bone doesn't seem to be broken.

Looking around the room, I attempt to gain my bearings. I seem to be in some kind of dusty old parlor. I can't tell if that means the room hasn't been used for a while or if that's just the way the interior decorator designed it when going for her "vampire-friendly" motif. The room is dark, but light seeps in through the cracked exit door. I let out a long sigh. I'm out of the frying pan, yes, but am I now into the fire? If the vampires stay-ing here couldn't be trusted when I *wasn't* sporting gaping wounds in my flesh, what will they be like now that I'm a walk-ing bloody billboard, thanks to Lassie out there?

But that can't be helped. I need to get to Jayden to check on him before the sun comes up and he goes to bed. To make sure he's okay. After all, I'm sure the powers-that-be will be none too pleased to open my bedroom door at dawn and learn I pulled a Houdini—leaving future visitation opportunities in question.

I hear laughter break out in the distance and remember what

Rufus told me. Jayden and the girls, giggling in the library. I manage to scramble to my feet and limp over to the door, pulling it open a crack and peeking through. There's no one in sight. So I slip through the door and out into the hallway. Following the sounds of laughter, I come to a set of French doors and steal a look into what indeed looks like a cozy library. There's a cheery fire raging in a mammoth stone fireplace, surrounded by floor-to-ceiling bookcases, stuffed with ancient-looking tomes. (And a few modern vampire bestsellers.) The girls are there, sitting on an old-fashioned Victorian sofa, all watching intently something going on across the room. Their eyes shine with excitement and Elizabeth is clapping her hands in glee.

Careening my neck, I strain to see what's gotten them so worked up. My eyes widen as they fall upon Jayden, attacking some young blond girl—biting her neck with wild abandon.

"No!" I cry, forgetting I'm supposed to be keeping a low profile. I dive into the room, rushing to his couch, attempting to drag him off his poor victim. But even in his half-vampire state, he's far too strong to budge.

"Jayden, stop!" I beg, feeling tears well into my eyes. "Don't do this!" After all, the Manor might overlook some "indiscretions," but I'm pretty sure my boyfriend will not. And I don't want to give him any more excuses to get rid of my friend.

To my surprise, Jayden releases his victim, turning to me, his mouth quirking up in a bloody grin. "Hey, Sunny!" he cries cheerfully. "Where have you been?"

I recoil in horror, tripping over a footstool and falling to the ground with a thump.

"Now, Jayden, it's not polite to talk with your mouth full," Elizabeth says primly.

"Sorry," Jayden replies, letting out a small burp. He covers his mouth in surprise and the three girls—make that four, including the blond girl he was just snacking on—start laughing.

"What the hell is going on here?" I demand, rubbing my butt.

Susan looks over at me. "Vampire lessons, of course," she sniffs.

I stare at her.

"Well, *someone's* got to train him, you know," Katie chimes in. "The guy doesn't even know how to properly drink from a donor."

"It's shameful," declares Elizabeth. "His Maker turning him and then just letting him loose like that. It's just not done."

"His Maker is dead," I say weakly, still horrified at the sight of Jayden with blood dripping from his mouth.

He wipes it on his sleeve and grins over at me, evidently super pleased with himself. "Now you don't have to worry about me accidentally hurting you," he announces, as if he's just discovered how to turn straw into gold. "I can drink and stop at will. Watch!" He turns to the blond girl. "Ready, Aleisha?" he asks.

"Yes, Master," she coos. "Bite me, baby!"

"It's okay! You don't have to," I quickly interject. "I get it, I believe you. Way to go."

He laughs. "Oh, and watch this!" he adds.

I squint at him. "Um, watch what?"

"You didn't see?" He sounds disappointed.

"Huh?" I am so lost here. "See what? You haven't done anything."

To my annoyance, the girls start laughing again.

"Jayden just ran around the room three times," Katie explains. "Not that someone like *you* could ever hope to see it."

"It's not her fault," Susan tells Jayden. "Her weak fairy eyes can't track super speed."

"I'm, like, the Speedy Gonzales of vampires!" Jayden chimes in. "It's one of my vampire powers. Cool, huh?"

"Um, sure," I mutter, feeling stupid and lame and out of place. "Congrats, I guess."

Jayden beams. "Maybe I'm not such a vampire failure after all, huh?"

"Failure!?" Elizabeth and Katie and Susan squeal all at once. "As if!"

"You make an amazing vampire!" Susan insists.

"It just takes time," adds Katie. "And training."

"And we're *just* the girls to teach you," Elizabeth finishes, possessively putting an arm around his shoulders. "Stick with us, kid. We'll make you into a super vamp."

"Super vamp!" Jayden exclaims. "I like the sound of that."

I feel sick to my stomach as I watch Elizabeth nuzzle up against him, as if he's her boyfriend or something. I know I have no right to say anything—Jayden and I are just friends—and I have Magnus. But at the same time, I have to admit it's killing me to see him so happy with another girl. I mean, it's not like I want him to be unhappy, of course. It's just . . .

Oh God, I'm totally losing it.

"Well, that's all fine and good," I manage to say, trying to push all the unwelcomed thoughts from my head. "But Jayden isn't going to need any of these lessons. 'Cause he's going to become mortal again—just as soon as Magnus brings back the Grail from Japan."

"If," Jayden corrects. "And I think that's a big if. To be honest, Sun, I don't think I'm very high on the guy's priority list."

My shoulders slump. I've been trying to keep the doubts from my head—trying to trust Magnus as he claims he deserves to be trusted. But at the same time, logic keeps rearing its ugly head. After all, even with the best intentions, could Magnus just tell the Consortium to shove their orders because he's still on the quest for the Holy Grail? I mean, that's like vampire treason. And as much as I want Jayden to have the chance to regain his humanity, I don't want Magnus to get in trouble, either. 'Cause I'm pretty sure the punishment for outright treason is death by stake.

It's not fair to put him in that position. To distract him from his important duties. Not when someone else could easily take over the task, freeing him up to concentrate on the war at hand.

Someone like the McDonald twins, for example.

"Jayden, can I talk to you for a minute?" I ask. "Alone?"

He looks up, surprised. "Of course," he says as he rises from his seat.

But Elizabeth stops him. "I don't think that's a good idea," she says. "After all, we were specifically told by your bodyguard not to let the two of you alone."

"In fact, if I remember right, I believe it was decided you should stay in your room," adds Katie. "Until morning."

Crap. In all the excitement, I forgot that I was still technically a prisoner. "Oh, right," I say quickly, before they can alert Rufus or the professor. "They let me out for a bathroom break. But I best be getting back! Sorry to disturb you guys. Have fun! I'll catch you later!"

Jayden looks at me, confused. "But, Sunny—"

I cut him off with a loud laugh. "Good luck with your lessons!" I tell him as I back out of the room. The girls watch me go with suspicious eyes, but thankfully none of them make a move to stop me. Once I'm far enough away for comfort I break out into a run, back toward the dusty parlor I came in from, to try to contemplate my next move.

How the hell am I going to get us out of here? I mean, just getting Jayden away from his own attractive jailers will be hard enough. And we probably aren't going to be able to just walk out the front door without being noticed. I'd use the window, but my friend Cujo is still outside, patiently awaiting my return. And while, once my wings are dry, I'll be able to fly again, that doesn't help Jayden at all. And I can't leave him here. Without my blood transfusions, he'll have no hope at all.

Voices in the hall interrupt my troubled thoughts. I duck behind a dusty armchair and hold my breath, praying they won't enter. But my prayers, it seems, are definitely not reaching the big guy tonight because a moment later the room floods with light and two vampires walk in and sit down.

And my ankle starts bleeding again.

10

"Are you sure you need to do this?" I hear the first vampire, who sounds like Professor Lucedio, ask the second as I try to put pressure on the wound. Vampires can smell blood a mile away, after all. Luckily, the professor is currently smoking a pipe, which is evidently masking the smell. But for how long?

I glance around for an exit, but the only one (besides the dog-guarded window) is across the room, past the two vampires. I'm basically stuck here until they leave. Or, you know, smell me and drain me dry.

I turn back to the conversation, not knowing what else to do. "After all, he's made great strides with the girls tonight," the professor is adding. "Maybe it's not too late to pull him in. I'm sure they would adopt the boy into their ranks. They seem quite fond of him, after all."

Wait—are they talking about Jayden?

The second vampire, who I realize is Tanner, the Blood Coven bodyguard, shifts uncomfortably in his seat. "I'm just following the Master's orders," he replies.

Ah, I get it. Professor Lucedio thinks Jayden should remain a vampire and join the English coven. But Tanner's telling him that Magnus instructed him to keep Jayden half human by giving him the blood transfusions until we find the cure. Good, Tanner. Play by the rules. Don't let those English vampires let you stray from the Master's orders . . .

"It just seems like such a waste," Lucedio adds. "A nice young vampire like that. And the girls have really taken to him, as well. Especially Elizabeth."

I scowl. Elizabeth doesn't deserve a nice vampire like Jayden. And Jayden would never go for a girl like her.

At least I hope not . . . Anyway, she won't have a chance, because I'm going to spring Jayden and we're going to find the Holy Grail and make him human again.

"I know, I know," Tanner replies. "But the situation is . . . complicated, as you know. In the end it'll be better this way."

Wait a second. What was that? I crane my neck, trying to determine what the vampires are doing. I catch a glimpse of Tanner, leaning over a coffee table, slipping a vial of clear liquid into a glass of blood.

What the—?

"And this will work?" Lecedio asks. "I don't want a big mess on my hands, you know. It'll disturb the other guests and I can't afford a big black mark on my Yelp rating in this economy."

Tanner stirs the blood. "It'll work, all right. And the autopsy will determine that his body simply rejected the transfusion and overtaxed itself fighting off enemy cells. His heart gives out, the abomination dies, and everyone can move on with their lives."

I clamp a hand over my mouth to stop my scream. They're going to kill Jayden and make it look like an accident. How could Tanner do something like this? And . . . wait . . . didn't he say he was following his Master's orders? But Magnus wouldn't do something so cold. Not after promising me he'd do everything he could to save Jayden's life . . .

"Well, it sounds like you have everything under control," Lucedio replies.

"I am only following Lord Magnus's orders," Tanner replies humbly. "He wanted a way to take care of the . . . problem . . . without upsetting . . . well, you know who."

My heart wrenches so hard for a moment I think it's going to break in two. Oh God. How could he? How could he lie to me like this? Tell me he's off to find the Grail and save Jayden's life while secretly instructing his bodyguard to kill the boy and make it look like an accident so I'd never suspect a thing.

And then having the nerve to lecture *me* about my trust issues.

Lucedio rises to his feet. "Speaking of the girl, I should go check on her. Poor thing. She's going to be devastated when she finds out her little friend is no more. She has quite a loyalty to the boy."

"Too much," Tanner adds bitterly. "Which is why we need to take care of this tonight."

The two vampires rise from their seats and start toward the door, leaving me shaking in fright. I have to get it together. Before they discover I'm missing and Tanner feeds Jayden the poisoned blood. I can be heartbroken at the betrayal later, once Jayden and I are safe. Right now I have to act.

Oh, Magnus, how could you? After all you said. After you begged me to trust you . . .

I shove the thoughts from my brain and start racking it for a solution. I can't fight them—I'm outnumbered and don't have vampire strength. I need to use fairy cunning instead.

And suddenly I realize exactly what I have to do.

11

"Hey, chaps, how's it bloody going?" I ask as I waltz into the library and don my best English accent. I plop down onto the sofa next to Jayden and grab a magazine off the coffee table, all casual-like. "What's Bonnie Prince Charles been up to these days, that jolly old hooligan? And oy, is that David Beckham hot or wot?"

Everyone stares at me and I do my best not to squirm, praying they can't see through my disguise. "Um, *Elizabeth*, have you been sampling the LSD-infused blood again?" asks Susan cautiously.

Good. They're buying it. Well, sort of. "Who, me?" I scoff. "Please. I don't need drugs to achieve this natural high."

"Darling, remember, what your sponsor said," Katie reminds me. "Denial is the first sign you have a problem. Do we need to get you to a meeting?"

Oh, Elizabeth has a problem, all right. But it has nothing to do with drugs. At least not at the moment. "Trust me, girls," I assure them, "it's all good in the hood. Drug-free is the way to be. Up with hope, down with dope. PCP is bad for me. And pot makes your brain rot, so I'd rather not." Ha. Wit is so my anti-drug.

The girls roll their eyes. "Whatever," Susan says. "But then what happened to the bottle of Edgar Allen Poe you were going to score us down in the blood cellar? The one we were going to use to teach Jayden the art of blood tasting?"

Oops. "Oh, right," I reply quickly. "Sorry, I forgot."

Susan shakes her head. "Great," she mutters. "I guess I'll go get it."

"No, no!" I interrupt quickly. The last thing I need is for them to go down there and discover the unconscious real Elizabeth tied up in the basement and realize that the girl they've been giving an intervention to is actually a shape-shifting fairy with bad acting skills and no drug problem whatsoever. "I'll get it." I turn to Jayden, who is creeping me out by staring at me with big puppy-dog eyes. It's a look I'm well familiar with because he used to use it only when looking at me. I mean, yes, technically he's still only looking at me this time around. But, like, Elizabeth me, not me, me.

Which, truth be told, makes me a little sad.

"Do you girls smell something?" Katie asks suddenly, wrinkling her nose in distaste. "It smells like . . . blood."

Susan nods. "Really sweet blood."

Crap. My ankle wound probably broke open again. Thankfully they can't see it, due to my disguise . . .

"Oh, I think that stupid fairy girl is wandering around again," I reply breezily. "Maybe you two should go after her and put her in her place."

The two girls look at one another. "Maybe we should . . ." Susan says.

"Yeah, she can't be just waltzing around here with an open sore like that," I remind them. "It's so not hygienic."

"Do you want to come with?" Katie asks me, as she rises from her seat. But I wave her off.

"No, no. I'll stay with Jayden here," I reply. "Keep him company."

The girls erupt into knowing giggles. "I bet you will," Susan teases.

"Have . . . fun . . ." adds Katie.

And with that, thankfully the two girls are out the door, leaving me alone with Jayden.

I turn to him. "Hey," I say, dropping the accent. "So we need to get—"

But I can't finish my sentence. Namely because suddenly I find Jayden's mouth on top of my own. Oh my God. He's kissing me. He's really kissing me. His soft lips hungrily moving against my own, exploring, tasting, sending shivers down to my very core. His hands reach into my hair, his fingers tangling in my curls.

Except I don't really have curls. And the lips he thinks he's kissing are not my own.

I shove him backward with such a force that he falls off the sofa. He looks up at me with wounded eyes as I rise to my feet, my hands on my hips, glaring down at him with fury.

"So, what? Are you guys, like, a couple now?" I demand, a flurry of emotions raging through me, too many to reconcile.

He scrambles to his feet, his face blazing. "I'm sorry," he babbles. "I just thought . . . from what you said before . . . I mean, I didn't mean to . . ."

It's all I can do not to shove him again. So hard he never gets up. "You dumbass," I rage. "I'm Sunny, not your girlfriend, Elizabeth."

He squints at me, uncomprehending. God, boys are so stupid. Always thinking with their you-know-whats.

"Sunny?" he repeats dumbly, his eyes still glazed over and lips still puffy from our kiss.

I shake my head, disgusted. "Yes. It's me. I just shape-shifted into Elizabeth so I could get the other girls to leave. It's one of my fairy powers."

"But . . . why?"

"'Cause you're in danger, Jayden. And I've got to get you out of here."

"What? No, I'm not. Everything's fine. In fact, it's been more than fine. The girls are so nice and I've been learning all about becoming a vampire . . ."

"Are you listening to a word I say?" I cry. "Your life is in danger. If you don't leave with me now, you'll be killed."

"But I thought vampires were immortal . . ."

I grit my teeth. Half of me just wants to leave him here at this point. But no. I have to be the bigger person.

"Look, lover boy, let's just say this so-called safe house isn't as safe as one might think," I reply, trying to still my temper. After all, he's not doing anything wrong. He's a single guy who likes a single girl and wants to hook up with her.

So why do I feel so betrayed?

I shake my head, trying to stay focused. "Any minute now, Tanner is going to come in here with your blood transfusion. Except this one will be laced with poison." I pause, then add, "They want to kill you, Jayden."

"But why would they want to do that? Why not just let me

become a vampire?" he asks. "I mean, Elizabeth's already suggested I come stay with them up north and join their coven."

Of course she has. "You just have to trust me," I reply. "We can talk more once we're free of this place."

He's silent, and for a moment I truly think he's going to turn down my offer of rescue. But eventually he nods his head, though still not looking me in the eye. "Okay," he says. "Lead the way."

And so I do, casually wandering through the halls with him, passing various vampire guests (who I catch sniffing the air suspiciously, but thankfully, they don't attack) until we reach the front door.

"Are you ready?" I ask, pulling out the Mini Cooper key I absconded from Elizabeth's pocket after knocking her out.

"As I'll ever be."

We make a run for the car, jumping in and peeling out of the driveway. As we go, we see Tanner running out the front door, waving the cup, a panicked look on his face.

"Master Jayden!" I hear him cry. "You need to take your blood!"

But I just step on the gas. Once we're a safe distance away, I shake off the glamour, returning to my own body again. Jayden stares at me with wide eyes. "It really is you!" he cries.

"Yes, I told you that."

He slumps back in his seat. "Which means I kissed you, not her," he moans. "This is so embarrassing. Don't tell Magnus, okay? I don't want to piss him off."

I scowl, my mind flashing back to the discussion I overheard with Tanner and Lucedio. Did Magnus really order Jayden to be killed? I want to trust that he wouldn't do something like that. But he's lied to me so many times before . . . And if he didn't think there was any way for me to find out . . .

I realize Jayden's still waiting for an answer.

"It's no big deal," I snarl, involuntarily reaching up to touch my fingers to my lips, still swollen from the accidental kiss. "Just don't do it again."

But even as I say the words, I wonder if I really mean them . . .

12

"Sunny!"

I run through the Tokyo security exit, throwing my arms around my sister in uncontained excitement. She squeezes me back, so tightly, for a moment I feel like I'm a half who's just managed to find her whole again.

"Oh, Rayne, it's so good to see you!" I cry. "Thank you so much for meeting me."

"Of course!" she exclaims. "How could I not, after what you told me on the phone? My God, what was Magnus thinking, leaving you there like that—with those horrible English bitches? Sometimes I do not know what goes on in that vampire's head."

Her words sober my enthusiasm. I've been wrestling with questions throughout the twelve-hour flight and I still haven't come up with any solid answers. Half of me wants to believe there has to be some other kind other explanation—like that Tanner was acting on his own, pretending to be following Magnus's orders or something. But why would the bodyguard bother to risk his hard-won Blood Coven membership and full-time job just to end some inconsequential vampire's life? It doesn't add up.

Unfortunately, the only other option, however, is that Magnus lied to me once again, after swearing he was trustworthy and actually getting mad at me for not trusting him. Sure, he probably had good intentions, knowing I'd never be able to let Jayden go without some kind of closure, even if that meant his actual death. Knowing him like I do, I can just picture his thought process now—realizing that finding the Grail in Tokyo would be like finding a needle in a haystack and that it would be kindest for all involved to just end things quietly and painlessly. So we could all move on. Except, you know, the guy he basically murdered in cold blood.

Seriously, if he lied to me again—even if he truly believed it was for my own good—if he ordered the death of my friend—he and I are done. Forever. End of story. No discussion.

"Hey, Rayne," Jayden says, walking up to the two of us. My sister regards him with a critical once-over.

"Hey, Jayden," she replies coolly. "You behave yourself on the flight? No snacking on the other passengers?"

Jayden holds up his hands and grins. "Total Vamp Scout," he says. "Though, to be honest, I wasn't very prepared. After all, Sunny yanked me out of Vampire Manor so fast I couldn't even make myself a nice to-go cup." He chuckles at his own joke. At least he seems to be feeling better, though he still refuses to look me in the eye.

"Don't worry, we'll find you some blood about town," Rayne assures him. "I'd lend you my donor, but I'm guessing you and Sunny need to keep a low profile here."

I nod. "Yes. If Magnus finds out I defied him and came here, he'll be so pissed," I tell her. Not to mention it would give him another opportunity to get rid of the competition. "Best to keep it all on the down-low."

"No problem," Rayne replies. "First we need to get you to your hotel. The vampires are all staying at this super amazing Park Hyatt in Shinjuku. It's where that old Bill Murray movie *Lost in Translation* was filmed. Completely luxe, with the most amazing views fifty-something stories up. You would have loved it."

"Sounds sweet. But we're not on vacation. We just need a place to crash."

"I know, I know." She waves me off. "You can't afford it anyway. And I already maxed out my personal credit card getting you your flights. Normally I'd have used my Blood Coven Black Amex, of course, but I didn't want Magnus's moronic secretary to see the charges and put two and two together."

"Right. So where are we going to stay then?"

She grins. "I scored you an awesome ryokan."

"A re-what?"

"A ryokan. It's like a traditional Japanese B and B. They originated back in 1603, during the Edo period."

"Please tell me they've renovated since then . . ."

"Come on," she says. "Grab your bags. We need to catch the next bullet train into town. It's like a forty-five-minute commute."

"How many days have you been here again?" I ask, impressed by her working knowledge of a city whose language looks like a five-year-old's scribbles to me.

"Only two," she confesses. "But I've been reading about Japan my whole life. It's only the coolest country ever, you know. So much culture, history . . ."

She's not fooling me whatsoever. "Um . . . Since when have *you* cared about culture? Or history, for that matter?"

She grins saucily. "Touché. To be honest, it's really all about the cosplay."

"The what?"

"You'll see . . ."

About an hour and a half later, we finally figure out our way via subway to the ryokan, which is nestled in a traditional urban Japanese neighborhood called Asakusa. The neighborhood is a fascinating mix of old and new and I can't stop staring at everything we pass. The main drag, I suppose, is not that different from New York City—except for the billion bicyclers crowding the streets—but behind it, the streets are narrow and crowded with a mixture of curio shops and tiny sushi bars alongside smoky karaoke booths and loud clanging "pachinko" parlors—where, according to Rayne, Japanese businessmen go to gamble. Neon lights blaze, intermixed with softer Japanese lanterns. There is also an obscene amount of vending machines, selling not only things like cigarettes, but girlie magazines, lingerie, and alcohol. Which should make things seem seedy. But actually everything's so freaking clean and bright it's hard to smell any degradation. For example, though there are zero trash cans anywhere in sight, there's also not a scrap of trash on the ground.

"Asakusa is best known for its Sensō-ji temple," Rayne, my tour guide, explains, as we take a right onto a narrow street, then an immediate left. "So you get a mix of tourists and neighborhood people here." She looks down at her map, then up at the building in front of us. "We're here!"

I have to admit, the ryokan is charming on the outside, like a quaint apartment building nestled on a quiet residential street. On its front porch is an old-fashioned rickshaw and I wonder if anyone actually still uses those today or if it's just a tourist thing like the bike rickshaws you see everywhere in New York and other cities.

We step inside the front door, into a small but cozy lobby, and are greeted warmly by the Okami, who is basically the landlady—or manager of the place. In halting English she welcomes us to the ryokan and has us sign the guest book.

"First time in Tokyo?" she asks kindly, making me immediately feel at home.

"Yes," I admit. "All of us."

"You need something, you let me know."

After we sign in, she hands me a long wooden bar with a key attached, much like the bathroom passes we get at school, and introduces us to an elderly Japanese gentleman who, she says, will show us to our room. We head up a tiny elevator and down a hall decorated with ancient-looking artwork and sculptures and stop outside a sliding wooden door. I grin at Rayne. This is pretty cool, I have to admit.

"Please. Your shoes," he instructs.

We take off our shoes and slip into wooden sandals. Then he slides open the door to our room. I'm exhausted at this point and cannot wait to throw myself onto a big cozy . . .

Um . . .

"Where's the furniture?" I demand as we step into a room not much bigger than the size of a double bed. Which would be fine, I suppose, if there were actually a double bed there. Instead, there's only a low wooden table on a woven straw floor, surrounded by multicolored cushions. I crane my neck to search out an actual bedroom—thinking maybe Rayne sprung for a suite—but all I see is a tiny sci-fi-looking toilet in the next room.

"Thanks," Rayne says to the host. "I think we're all set here." He bows and makes his exit.

"What the hell, Rayne?" I demand, looking around the room.

"I told you, this is a ryokan," my sister reminds me. As if that should make me feel better. "It's a traditional Japanese—"

"Yeah, yeah, I get it," I interrupt grumpily. I'm tired and frustrated and can't believe there's no place to sleep. "But why no bed? Didn't traditional Japanese people have to get a good night's sleep, too? And why is it so tiny?"

Rayne rolls her eyes. "It's a small island, Sunny. They've got to make room for everyone."

Right.

"Whoa, that toilet is cool," Jayden says, coming out of the bedroom. "There's, like, a water fountain button on it."

"It's a built-in bidet," Rayne informs him. "So I hope to God you didn't drink out of it."

"And where's the shower?" I demand, peeking into the bathroom.

"Um." Rayne bites her lower lip. "Well, traditionally they used public baths . . ."

Oh my God, I am seriously going to kill her.

"Look, it's not that bad," she protests. "You move the table aside when you want to sleep. And there are futons—here in this closet—that you pull out and sleep on." She looks up at me, her eyes shining. "Come on, you have to admit, it's kind of cool, right? Like you're living in authentic ancient Japan."

"Please. Cool is sleeping at the Park Hyatt on a fluffy bed

with Egyptian cotton linens," I point out. "Not glorified indoor camping with no shower."

Rayne scowls. "Where's your sense of adventure?"

"Sorry, I guess the dog ate it, along with half my ankle while I was narrowly escaping for my life back in England."

From out the window we can hear a man burst into very bad karaoke song. Awesomeness.

"Look, you just need a good night's sleep is all." Rayne points out the obvious. "The sun's almost up, after all, and Jayden looks like he's about to pass out."

Jayden stops, mid-yawn, snapping his mouth closed. "Sorry," he says sheepishly.

"Okay, fine," I say with a scowl. "We'll stay here for now. But you've got to find us a regular non-traditional hotel for tomorrow. Also some kind of blood supply for Jayden. Or else he's going to end up snacking on that karaoker out there. Which, I suppose, wouldn't be totally awful, come to think of it."

"What about giving him some of yours to tide him over?"

I glance down at my bruised and battered arm. "I would. But one, we left England in such a hurry I didn't have time to retrieve the draining kit. And two, my supply's more than a bit low. I'm thinking I might like to save a tiny bit for myself to use on those pesky little bodily functions like heartbeat and circulation and stuff."

"Right." Rayne plops down on a cushion and plugs in the electric teakettle on the table. "Well, I can't get any from the Blood Coven, that's for sure. It's tightly rationed when you're overseas and they'd be sure to ask questions. What we really need is some kind of Blood Bar. Like the one I infiltrated back in the spring."

I sit down across from her, cross-legged. "Do they have those here?" I ask eagerly, forgetting for a moment I'm mad at her. "Do you know where one is?" Maybe my sister's nerdy Japan fetish will actually pay off for once.

But no, she shakes her head. "Let me do a little Googling," she says, pulling her iPad out of her bag.

"Oh, cool, is that ancient Japanese Wi-Fi you're logging into there?" I ask sarcastically.

"Shush, you Ugly American, and drink your damn tea."

I glance over at Jayden, who's slunk into a corner of the room, staring down at his hands. "Are you okay?" I ask.

He looks up at me with hollow eyes. "Just . . . hungry . . ." he confesses. "You may want to keep your distance."

My heart aches for him and suddenly I can't be mad anymore. He's gone through so much in the past few days. "I'm sorry," I say, crawling over to him. "I know it's been an awful week. But I promise we're going to figure this out, okay? I'm not going to give up. We'll get you turned back into a human, if it's the last thing I do."

He gives me a hopeful smile. "Oh, Sunny," he says. "What would I do without you?" And my heart breaks all over again.

"Well, you'll never have to worry about that," I assure him firmly, so as not to crumble into a teary mess. I reach out to squeeze his hand.

"Okay, lovebirds, listen up," Rayne interrupts. "I've found something that might work."

"Oh?" I crawl over to her and look down at the iPad. "The Vampire Café? Are you kidding me?"

Rayne chuckles. "It's a theme restaurant. Supposed to be like Dracula's lair or something. But according to some of the vampire forums I just read, they supposedly have real blood on tap for the more . . . discriminating customer."

"That's awesome. Thanks, Rayne!" I turn to Jayden. "What do you think?"

But my friend is already passed out cold. I glance out the window. Sure enough, the first rays of sun are peeking through. I rise from my seat and pull the bamboo blinds closed.

"I guess he's out for the day," I tell my sister. "So we'll hit the café tonight, if that works for you."

Rayne nods. "I'll do my best to sneak away," she says. "But for now, I've got to get back to the Park Hyatt. They've got me and Jareth on day-missions, since none of the other vampires can go out then." She glances at her watch. "My shift starts in less than an hour."

As she rises to her feet I step over to hug her. "Thank you," I say. "And I'm sorry I complained about the accommodations. They're really quite charming, to be honest."

"It's okay. I'm used to you being the lame twin," she teases as she hugs me back. I shove her away playfully.

"Now get the hell out of here and let me sleep."

And so she climbs out of the room, sliding the door shut behind her. I reach into the closet to pull out the futon mattresses. Once I've got them set up into a cozy little nest, I drag Jayden's sleeping figure onto one of them and pull a down comforter over his body, to further block out any stray rays of light. Then I curl up onto the other mat beside him and close my eyes.

But tired and jet-lagged as I am, I can't sleep. And so I lie there, watching Jayden toss and turn in restless slumber.

"Sunny," he murmurs in his sleep. "Oh, Sunny . . ."

My heart full, I reach out and lay a hand on his arm, hoping my touch will soothe him, even in his sleep. A moment later, it seems to work and his body relaxes into a deeper phase of rest. I watch him for a while longer, taking in his tousled hair and sooty lashes brushing against his pale skin. He looks so innocent, so sweet. How could I have even thought to be mad at him?

"I'm going to make this work," I promise him softly as my own body succumbs to my exhaustion at last. "I refuse to make you pay for my mistakes."

13

The Vampire Café is located in the Ginza neighborhood of Tokyo, which is about as opposite of Asakusa as you can get. I'm talking luxury boutiques—Chanel, Louis Vuitton, Gucci, and a twelve-story (!) Abercrombie and Fitch. If Jayden weren't so hungry, I'd so be shopping like a fiend.

We took the subway here and had a car almost all to ourselves after getting on and having Jayden shake and shiver like a heroin addict. He woke up with major blood withdrawal and it's been getting worse ever since. Some Japanese women wearing surgical masks over their mouths gave him dirty looks before exiting to another car. Sadly, I couldn't very well explain to them that vampirism isn't exactly an airborne virus they could catch.

We meet up with Rayne outside the Ginza-itchōme Station, entering a world of bright lights and tall skyscrapers, to which my sister immediately turns up her nose in disgust. I think from her research she assumed Japan was one big charming manga full of boys and girls wearing cat ears, not a neon version of Fifth Avenue.

"Come on," I say, grabbing her arm. "We've got to hurry."

After wandering around a bit—Tokyo addresses are almost impossible to decipher, due to the fact that they're based on a block system, rather than street address—we finally locate the building that houses the Vampire Café.

The three of us board the elevator and it slides open into a dark, mysterious restaurant. A Japanese hostess, dressed in a French maid's uniform, greets us at the door and leads us inside.

Rayne lets out a low gasp as we step into the restaurant's interior. The place is like her dream bedroom. All decked out in black and crimson with Gothic candelabras offering low mood lighting. In the center of the room is a life-sized, old-fashioned coffin, adorned with skulls and roses, and the black carpet has big red splotches that I guess are supposed to represent bloodstains.

Now, as you know, I myself am totally not into the whole Goth esthetic at all, but I have to admit, this place is pretty awesome, with many of the tables enclosed by red velvet curtains to give diners a sense of ultimate privacy. Our hostess leads us over to one of them, pulling back the curtains and allowing us to slide into our seats before closing the curtains once again, leaving us in a kind of cozy little cave. On the table are bloodred napkins, chopsticks, a candle, and a brass bell.

"If only Jareth were here," Rayne swoons. "This is, like, the most romantic restaurant ever."

"We're not here for the five-star dining," I remind her. "Especially since two out of the three of us can't even eat food."

"Yeah, yeah. Step on my rapture, why don't you?"

I open my mouth to tease her some more, but at that moment

the curtains part and a man, dressed in a butler's uniform, starts chattering at us in rapid Japanese.

"No, no!" Rayne interrupts. *"No habla Japanese."*

"That's Spanish, you moron," I point out, pulling the phrase book I bought at the airport out of my bag and frantically paging through.

"Eigo wo hanashimasu ka?" Do you speak English?

"*Hai!* A little," he replies, looking excited but unsure. "You are American?"

We nod.

"You like blood . . . cocktail?" he asks.

Rayne gives me an excited glance. "Yes, please!" she says. "Two cups."

"I'll just take . . . um . . . *mizu*," I add, after looking up the Japanese word for water. No blood for this fairy, thank you very much.

The waiter nods and backs away, the curtains slipping shut behind him. Rayne turns to Jayden and me, an ecstatic look on her face. "Oh my God, that was easier than I thought!" she gushes. "I guess I shouldn't expect anything less from Tokyo. It's so much cooler than the United States. I mean, they don't even try to hide the fact that they're serving vampires here, like Club Fang has to do back home." She reaches out and grips Jayden's forearm. "So awesome, huh?" she asks him. "We'll get you fixed up in no time!"

The waiter returns a moment later with two dainty wineglasses filled with red liquid and my cup of water. Rayne and Jayden grab their drinks and each take an eager sip. Then they look at each other and set down their cups in apparent disgust.

"What?" I ask. "Not your blood type?"

"It's wine," Rayne replies in an overwhelmingly disappointed voice. "Like, real wine." She looks up at the waiter. "I thought you said it was blood." When the waiter looks back at her blankly, she grabs my phrase book from me and starts paging through. "*Chi?*"

The waiter nods and points to the glass. "*Chi,*" he assures her with a wide, naive smile. "You no like it?"

Rayne sets down her glass, looking bummed. "No, I like it fine. It's just not what I expected is all."

The waiter shrugs, then scurries away, probably lamenting the fact he got stuck with the American table tonight. Rayne watches him go, scowling. "Wine," she repeats scornfully.

"Come on, Rayne, what did you expect?" I ask. "This is a real restaurant. They're not just going to have blood on the menu. The Japanese health department would shut them down in a heartbeat, I'm sure." I pull open the curtain to spy on the rest of the place. In a corner, a group of Japanese teens are having what appears to be a birthday party, complete with "bleeding" raspberry cake. "Face it. This place is just a tourist trap, not a real vampire den."

Rayne bites her lower lip. "That's just their cover," she says, unwilling, evidently, to give up. Her eyes scan the room. "The forums said they have blood on tap. Maybe it's not in the main restaurant. Maybe they have a back door into a secret room. I don't suppose your phrase book has how to say 'blood bar' in Japanese, does it?" She starts looking through the book again.

"Sure, it's right after 'Where's the bathroom?' in their list of top useful phrases," I reply dryly. Rayne throws the book at my head.

At that moment, the waiter returns with our first course. Some kind of shrimp appetizer, swaddled in a plastic coffin and dripping in bloodred cocktail sauce. Genuine or no, I give this place an A+ for presentation.

"Do you know any vampires?" Rayne asks the poor waiter, evidently done with any attempts to speak his native tongue.

"Vampire!" He nods enthusiastically.

Rayne's eyes light up. "Where?"

He cocks his head in confusion, then makes a sweeping gesture around the restaurant. "Vampire . . . Café!" he says slowly, as if speaking to a dim-witted child. Which, of course, in this case isn't far off the mark.

Rayne lets out a frustrated breath. "Well, where's the back room? I heard there's a Blood Bar here. Where's the entrance to that?" She's practically shouting now, falling into the trap so many tourists do—assuming that if they only speak louder, they'll suddenly be understood.

But our waiter only looks baffled. "Bath-room?" he tries. Poor guy.

"No, no! I mean—"

"It's okay," I cut her off. "We're fine," I tell the waiter. "*Domo arigato*. Thank you."

The waiter looks relieved and babbles something in Japanese that I assume is "Enjoy your meal" but very well could be "Go back to McDonald's, you stupid American pigs." I poke my appetizer with a chopstick, then take a tentative bite. Hmm, not bad. I chase it with Rayne's glass of wine and then steal her appetizer off her plate. "Too bad you guys can't eat," I tell the two sulking vampires across from me. "This is pretty good."

"A vampire restaurant is the stupidest idea ever," my sister grumps. "Seeing as real vampires don't eat." She slumps back into her chair with a huff. "Maybe we should have tried somewhere else." She pulls the curtain back, as if she wants to just leave then and there. I'm about to tell her that she can't just up and walk away on the bill and, besides, I want to finish my meal, but then

I notice that the birthday party people are all looking at us, and whispering furtively to one another. I also notice that none of them seem to be actually eating any of the cake in front of them, but the red sauce has been drained dry.

And they all have identical glasses of red wine.

"Rayne," I hiss. "Take a look at that group over there."

Rayne stops climbing out of the booth and looks over in the direction of the party. "What, more stupid tourists? Who cares?"

"Yeah, but they keep looking at us and whispering."

"Whatever. I'm so—" Rayne cuts off as she does a double take. "Wait a second," she hisses. "Is that . . ." Her eyes widen in recognition. "Oh my God, it is! What the hell is *he* doing here?"

14

"Who?" I ask, trying to peek back through the curtains for someone recognizable at the party table, praying it's not a member of the Blood Coven. But before I can scan the crowd, my sister yanks me back inside the booth.

"Race Jameson," she hisses. "He's sitting at the far end of the table."

"What?" I stare at her. "Are you sure?"

"Of course I'm sure. I spent thirty days in lockup with Mr. Vampire Rock Star. I'd recognize him anywhere. I totally forgot that he's here on some Japanese comeback tour now that he's off the bad blood."

"Cool." I try to part the curtains again. "We should totally say hi. Do you think he'll remember me from the time he helped us with the werewolves?"

My sister pulls the curtains shut again. "No."

"No, you don't think he'll remember?"

"No, I don't want to say hi."

"But why?" I protest. "He's totally nice. Not to mention he's a vampire. He might know where we can get Jayden some blood."

Jayden looks up hopefully.

But my sister shakes her head. "I don't care if he's walking around with an IV blood drip permanently fused to his veins. We're not going over there."

I narrow my eyes at her. "Rayne, what happened in rehab?"

But before she can tell me to mind my own business, our curtain parts. At first I assume it's the waiter, coming back with the second course, but the piercing violet-colored eyes prove me wrong.

"Well, well, if it isn't the Bobbsey Twins," Race Jameson purrs in a velvety voice. "What on Earth are you doing here in Japan?"

"That would be the McDonald twins and none of your business," Rayne retorts, refusing to look him in the eye.

"Aw, don't be like that, my little Rayney Day," he says as he plops down beside my sister. She scoots to the other half of the booth, as far away from the rock star as she can get. "I thought we were friends."

"Yeah, and I thought the Tooth Fairy was real," my sister snarls. "Until, you know, I stopped believing in fairy tales."

"Um, actually the Tooth Fairy is real," I remind her. "In fact, Mom says she's our third cousin twice removed."

Race turns to me. "And there she is, the Sunshine of my life," he coos. "You're looking particularly fine this evening." He sniffs the air. "And you smell divine. What is that scent you're wearing?"

"Eau du fairy." I giggle, tossing my hair over my shoulder,

feeling my cheeks flush with sudden heat. Mmm. Race Jameson is so hot. Sooo hot. With his razor-cut black hair and skintight leather pants and . . . those eyes. Those gorgeous, unnatural, glowing purple—

"Uh, yo, Mr. Rock Star," my sister interrupts. "No vampire scenting my sister."

Race's blazing eyes dim instantly, as if someone turned off a light switch. He scowls. "Aw, come on, babe. I was just having a bit of fun."

I shake myself, my warm glow fading like Race's eyes, replaced by the itchy feeling of little creepy crawlies running up and down my arms. Is that what the vampire scent feels like? Yuck. I look up at Race. Okay, fine. He's still hot. But at least I no longer have the undying urge to crawl across the table and sit in his lap. So that's something.

"There is no fun to be had here," Rayne assures him. "At least not with my dear twin. Besides, I thought you were cured of that kind of thing. You know, twelve steps and all that?"

"I'm taking it one day at time," he growls in a throaty voice. "And hey, how do you know this is just a random blood grab, anyway? Maybe I want to make your sister my eternal blood mate. To spend every moment of my life wrapped in her loving arms . . ."

"You know, I should have just let you take a sip," my sister says, shaking her head in disgust. "Her Holy Grail–tainted blood would have put you out of your misery for good."

Race holds up his hands. "Okay, okay, fine. I promise. No drinking from your blood relatives. But you still haven't told me why you're here in Tokyo. And if you don't, I'm going to assume you're stalking me like the rabid fan girl you are."

"Please. I'd rather stalk Justin Bieber."

"Oh, dear little Justin Bieber," Race croons. "If only I could get close enough to make him one of us. Tween girls for generations to come would forever be in my debt."

Rayne rolls her eyes. "Okay, fine. We're on the quest for the Holy Grail, if you must know."

"Uh . . ." Race raises an eyebrow. "The cup of Christ? You think it's here in Godzilla land?"

"It was stolen," I pipe in. "And my friend Jayden here needs it." I motion to Jayden, who's been sitting, staring at the singer with awestruck eyes, which I'm hoping is due to the fact he's never been in such close proximity to a rock God before and not Race vampire scenting him on the sly. Though can vampires even vampire scent other vampires? I still have no idea.

"You haven't seen a group of Alpha flunkies hanging around the city, have you?" Rayne asks. "They'd be wearing red cloaks."

Race shakes his head. "Sorry," he says, actually sounding like he is, for once. "But I can keep an eye out for you." His upper lip quirks into a half grin. "Give me your phone number and I'll call you the second I hear anything."

"Yeah, right. You're not getting my digits that easy."

Race puts on a hurt look again. "Oh, Rayney Day, you slay me."

"If only it were that easy."

I shake my head. They can banter all night. But Jayden looks like he's going to pass out at any moment. "Look, Race," I interject, "Jayden here is in desperate need for blood. We came here thinking there was some kind back-door Blood Bar here, but we're totally striking out with the waiter. Can you help?"

Race grins. "Now, why didn't you just say so?" he admonishes

Rayne. "While the Holy Grail is out of even my illustrious, far-reaching grasp, I can certainly hook you up with some blood. Just come back to my hotel room and I'll—"

"Absolutely not."

"Oh fine," he pouts. "There's a Blood Bar in this restaurant, yes. But it's highly protected. And they're not going to just let in any old vampire without going through the proper channels." He scratches his head. "But let me see what I can do." He rises from his seat and heads back over to the party table, whispering something to one of his companions. The girl, Japanese and utterly lovely, gives us a hard look, then shakes her head. Race whispers some more.

"It's lucky we found him," I observe, watching the scene.

"I could think of other words."

I turn to my sister. "What is it with the two of you, anyway?"

"Nothing. I just find him pretty much the most annoying vampire to walk the face of the Earth."

"But why? He seems so harmless."

"Sunny, don't be fooled. His bite is much worse than his bark."

Race returns to our table. "Okay," he says. "I talked to Suki. She says this Blood Bar's velvet rope is the tightest in town. Only celebs and politicians even have a chance. But she thinks maybe she can score you a guest pass to the Harajuku Bite Club tomorrow night. Can you wait that long?"

The two of us look at Jayden. He nods weakly. "I think so," he says.

"I guess we have no choice," Rayne adds. "So what, we meet back here?"

Race shakes his head. "The girls over there belong to the Cosplay Coven." He hands Rayne a folded piece of paper. "Here's the address. Suki wants you to meet them after sundown. They'll take you to Bite Club from there. Unfortunately," he adds, "I have a concert tomorrow night. I won't be able to join you."

"How tragic," Rayne mutters.

I look over at the girls, who are watching with curious expressions on their faces. "Are you sure we can trust them?" I ask.

Race grins cockily. "Do you have any choice?"

15

After plopping down a huge tip for the waiter, the three of us exit the restaurant. (And are subsequently chased down by said waiter, who hands me back my extra *yen*. Turns out the whole tipping thing in Japan is not done. In fact, it can be seen as a sign of dishonor. Weird, huh? Personally, if I were him, I'd just take the money and run. Especially after having to deal with my annoying twin sister. He earned his money that night, big-time, just for not spitting in her drink.)

We say our good-byes to Rayne, who jumps in a cab to cut west across town and get back to Shinjuku and her luxury hotel. Jayden and I, on the other hand, are back on the subway, heading toward our little ryokan. Rayne did offer to try to get us a new reservation at a nearby Best Western, I but figured it was easier to just stay where we are at this point. Besides, I have to admit, the place is growing on me. Like a cozy little nest for just the two of us.

Jayden sleeps for most of the subway ride and then listlessly shuffles down the main road toward the ryokan. I study him worriedly as we stop at a crosswalk. Under the streetlights, his skin looks almost translucent and the hollows under his eyes are as deep as the Grand Canyon. When we get back to our room, he plops down on the futon mat in exhaustion.

"How are you feeling?" I ask worriedly.

He looks up, trying to put on a brave face. "Fine."

"You don't look fine. You look terrible."

"Thanks."

I climb onto my own futon, propping myself on my side with my elbow. "You know what I mean," I protest, poking him playfully. Just a small tap, but it nearly knocks him over. My teasing face sobers. "Seriously, Jayden. Are you going to make it 'til tomorrow?"

He rolls onto his back and stares up at the low ceiling. "I don't have any choice, do I?"

"I don't know. Maybe I could try to catch you a rat or something. They've got to have rats here, right? Even though, to be honest, I don't know what they'd eat, the streets are so freaking clean . . ."

"I don't want a rat, Sunny."

"A cat? Though I think they might be sacred here. Or lucky. I guess it'd be lucky to find a cat to feed you . . ."

Jayden manages to throw a pillow at me.

I sigh. This sucks. And I can't even feed him my own blood, because the whole syringe/blood bag thing is back in England.

Unless . . .

"Jayden," I say softly.

For a moment I think he's already fallen asleep. Then I hear a quiet. "Yeah?"

"What about my blood?"

"I thought you said you were too low."

"I feel much better today. I think I can give a little."

"But we don't have the syringe."

"I know but . . . what if you took it the old-fashioned way?"

His eyes widen. "I couldn't. I mean, remember what happened last time? And here there'd be no Magnus to save you . . ."

I swallow hard, wondering if I'm sure what I'm saying. Once I make the offer, there's no turning back. But if I don't, I'm not sure Jayden will live through the night.

"Well, you've had training since then," I remind him. "You had no problem sampling from that girl back at the coven and letting her go afterward."

"Yeah, sure, but I don't love *her*," Jayden blurts out.

Wait—what? What did he just say? My heart starts pounding in my chest with the intensity of an 808 drum. "Jayden—"

His pale face pinkens. If he wasn't a vampire, I imagine he'd be tomato red at this point. "Never mind," he says quickly. "I can probably drink from you. If you're willing to risk it, that is."

At this point, I'm scarcely interested in the drinking discussion. I want to know more about his slip of the tongue. Does he really love me? What about Elizabeth? If he does love me, why did he kiss her? Well, kiss me thinking he was kissing her. But if he loved me he wouldn't have tried to do that, right? Unless somehow deep inside he knew it *was* me, but pretended he didn't so he could kiss me without any consequence.

This is so confusing. I shake my head. *Don't go there, Sunny.* Why torture him and make him admit something that won't do him any good? Loving me is probably a noose around his neck right about now. And if I press the issue, I'll probably end up choking him.

So I let it go. But inside, I have to admit, I do feel a little warmer.

"Okay, let's do this," I tell him, back to the matter at hand. "Um, where do you want to bite? My arm? My leg?"

He manages to sit up on his mat, looking at me with sleepy green eyes, framed by lashes way too long for a boy. Smiling shyly, he points at my neck.

I bite my lower lip. "There? Really?"

He shrugs. "The blood there is the most powerful, according to the girls," he says simply. But I wonder, suddenly, if he's telling the whole truth about that.

I guess it doesn't matter. "Okay," I say, my hands shaking as I pull back my hair. I draw in a deep breath. "Okay. Whenever you're ready, I'm—"

I gasp. Unable to finish my sentence as he leans into me, taking me firmly into his arms and pressing his face to my neck. At first it tickles, the brush of lips against sensitive skin. Then there's a sting.

And then there's the ecstasy.

My head swims in rapture as sunlight flames around me in the middle of the dark room. Heavy warmth envelops me, stealing my breath. A thousand fingers tangling through my hair. My toes curl, my mouth gapes. My eyes roll to the back of my head. I'm like a new baby come into the world. But at the same time, the oldest, wisest soul leaving it behind. I'm a wild deer, running free through an emerald forest. A sleek silverfish diving into the ocean's depth. A giant bird, soaring through the crystal-blue sky.

"Oh, Jayden," I murmur huskily.

Suddenly the light turns off. The glow fades, the feeling ends. And I'm back in the small, cramped ryokan. Back to the girl I always was.

"Oh my God," I cry, reaching up to feel my neck. "That was incredible. Even better than the first time." I shiver. The room suddenly seems to have dropped in temperature about twenty degrees and I'm desperate to get that warmth back. I crawl after Jayden, who's retreated to the other end of the room and is hugging his knees together, a distraught look on his face and a drop of blood dripping down his chin.

"Jayden, you stopped too soon," I tell him. "I have plenty left. Drink some more. Come on."

He scowls. "I'm not thirsty anymore."

"What?" My heart wrenches with a sudden, startling sense of abandonment. "Of course you are. You didn't drink nearly enough. I understand you didn't want to go too far, but instead you left too soon. Drink some more. Please." I know I'm begging, but I can't help it. All I can think about are his gorgeous fangs, attached firmly to my neck.

"I'm *fine*, Sunny," he asserts. "Just go to sleep."

"Jayden, you're being unreasonable here! I have plenty more blood to give."

"Then go give it to someone else, you crackhead," he mutters, getting up and walking out of the room, sliding the door shut loudly behind him. In the distance, I can hear his heavy footsteps stomp down the hall.

What on Earth did I do to make him so mad?

16

"Are you ready yet?" I call out to my sister, who's locked herself in the tiny ryokan bathroom for the last forty-five minutes. For someone who supposedly scorns all things fashion, she sure takes a long time picking out her outfits.

The door opens. Rayne pokes her head out, her black hair sticking out at every angle. She catches sight of me and scowls. "Sunny, you're still in your pajamas. How can you ask me if I'm ready?"

"Please. I'll be ready in five minutes, if I could just gain access to the bathroom."

Rayne clicks her teeth in disapproval. "Didn't we go over this already? You can't just wear your boring old jeans and flip-flops when visiting real Harajuku vampires. If you're not dressed like some manga or anime character, they're going to think you're an outsider."

"Right. Because my blond hair and American accent won't have already given that away."

Rayne sighs. "Come on, Sun," she begs. "Try to be a good sport. We're infiltrating a foreign vampire coven here. At least try to play the part."

"You know," I say, "this is strangely reminiscent of that first night at Club Fang when you talked me into wearing a BITE ME T-shirt to 'blend in.' Do I have to remind you how *that* turned out?"

Rayne rolls her eyes and retreats back to the bathroom. I glance over at Jayden and grin. He laughs and shakes his head.

Early that morning, just before sunrise, he returned to the ryokan, full of apologies and regret for leaving like he did. I, in turn, apologized for my own weird addictlike response to his blood drinking and we both decided drinking blood from the source was just a bad idea for everyone involved and the next time he needed a fix, we'd get it through a needle again. After more murmured apologies we fell asleep, side by side, only to wake up at dusk with my sister banging on the door. There was still more to be said—like addressing those three little words hanging over our heads like an elephant in the room, for example—but they'd have to wait. First, he needed his blood.

A few minutes later, Rayne flounces out of the bathroom, wearing a gorgeous short red-and-black kimono-like dress, fluffed out with large petticoats. Her hair has been straightened to an inch of its life and her copious black eye makeup is stunning. I have to admit, she made the most of her time in there.

Jayden gives a low whistle. "Wow, Rayne, you look hot," he teases.

My sister's cheeks color into a blush. "Well, when in Rome," she says. "Or in Tokyo, Japan, in this case."

"Well, now that you're done, let's talk about me," I say with a small grin, a delicious plan forming in my mind. I grab her iPad and hand it over to her. "Show me the kind of outfit you think I should be wearing."

She grabs the iPad and sits down on the floor, cross-legged, firing up Google Images and typing in "Harajuku Cosplay." The screen fills with Japanese teens in colorful costumes. Boys with oversized prop swords and spiky blue hair. Girls with lacy dresses and parasols, holding up signs that read FREE HUGS! Manga characters come to life. I have to admit, they look pretty cool.

"How about her?" I ask, pointing to a picture of a girl in frilly pink-and-white dress with a big bow in her hair. The caption underneath her reads SWEET LOLLI, and she's way more my style than some of the Gothy-looking ones.

Rayne peers down at the photo. "Sure," she says with a shrug. "I mean, she'd be perfect, of course. But unless you went out for a daytime shopping spree after I left you, I'm guessing you don't own—"

I snap my fingers. Rayne and Jayden stare at me, mouths agape.

"Oh my God," my sister gasps.

"How'd you do that?" Jayden adds.

I fluff up my new golden curls and straighten my flouncy dress, enjoying their shocked faces. "Fairy powers are so useful when it comes to keeping up with fashion trends."

"You can shape-shift?" Rayne cries.

I nod. "Of course, I need to have a point of reference. A person, a photo . . ."

"That is so not fair! All I got for stupid fairy powers is the inability to lie. Which, obviously, isn't a power at all, but a crippling weakness that is bound to bring about my doom."

I laugh, scrambling to my feet. "Poor Rayne. Life's so tough for you." I walk over to the door. "Now come on, let's head to Harajuku!"

We crisscross the city by subway and exit at Harajuku Station. Rayne's practically dancing in excitement as she gapes at all the teens in their costumes. It's so strange how they just congregate here. Like a living, breathing art exhibit for all the tourists to see. And the variety in their outfits is mind-boggling. From giggling girls in pretty light pink and blue dresses, similar to my own, to scary girls in gas masks and military gear. Most are wearing brightly colored wigs, but some of them have sculpted their own hair into manga-esque spikes that defy gravity. Almost all of them carry rollaway bags, which I assume means they changed into their costumes in a nearby bathroom, not at home, for their parents to object.

"This is so cool," Rayne breathes, her eyes darting from group to group, as if desperate to take in every detail. "Why don't people do this in America?"

"Come on," I say, grabbing her arm. "We can do the tourist thing later. Right now we have to find Race's friends and get Jayden some blood." I glance back at my friend. He's already lost some of the color he gained from my blood the night before and definitely looks in need of a refill.

My sister nods and pulls out her hand-drawn map. "Okay," she says. "According to this, we have to head down Takeshita Dori here. She points to a narrow pedestrian-only street milling with Japanese teens. "It's on a small street off the main drag."

Jayden and I follow her lead and soon we're dodging tourists in a kind of outdoor mall, with two stories of storefronts selling everything from sundresses and thigh-high stockings to dark, bondage-looking Goth gear, complete with metal buckles and shiny studs. We pass bubble tea shops galore, a McDonald's, and street carts selling about a billion varieties of crepes. There are also a ton of clothing shops, selling T-shirts with English phrases that just don't make any sense. Of course, Japanese kids probably feel the same way when they come to America and see everyone with kanji tattoos that are supposed to mean "peace" and "Zen" but probably really mean "stupid" and "naive."

"Hang on a second," I cry to Rayne and Jayden, over the bad '70s American rock spilling out over the airways. I stop at the crepe shop and pick out a strawberry-and-crème-flavored one. As a fairy, my sweet tooth has grown about 300 percent and I crave sugar as much as vampires crave blood. And luckily, as a fairy, I'll never gain an ounce, no matter how much I eat, thanks to a magical nectar elixir fairy scientists concocted that literally dissolves fat cells. Meaning fairies can eat all they want—and never have to count carbs.

Which is good, seeing as right now, as Jayden's blood donor, I need all the nutrients I can get.

Once I get my dessert, the three of us cut behind the main drag and into a small, unassuming neighborhood. It's hard to believe just walking a street over can make such a difference in atmosphere. Here, small houses and apartment buildings line the quiet streets.

"This is the place," Rayne says, stopping in front of a small cinder-block home. It's boxy and ugly, styled in a sort of '80s modern design. So not the type of place I'd imagine a Japanese vampire coven to call home.

My sister rings the bell and a moment later, a little girl, probably about nine years old, answers the door and bows low. *"Kon-*

banwa," she greets solemnly, which I remember from my phrase book means "Good evening."

"Oh, I'm sorry," I say, a little taken aback. The girl is dressed like a Japanese schoolgirl—the real kind, not the slutty manga kind—and has her hair parted into two silky braids. "We must have the wrong place . . ."

"Rayne? Sunny? Jayden?" The girl squeals in a high-pitched but perfectly spoken English. She bounces up from her bow as if her feet were made of springs. "So glad to meet you! Race has told me so much about you." She smiles widely, revealing a set of blindingly white fangs.

Whoa. I glance at my sister, shocked beyond belief. This is only the second time I've ever seen a child vampire in real life. They're extremely rare and totally illegal—at least in the United States. In fact, Slayer Inc. sees them as an abomination and is always trying to wipe their kind off the face of the Earth.

"My name is Amaya," the girl adds, tossing her long black braid over her shoulder. "It means 'night rain.'" She winks at my sister. "We have much in common, you and I."

The look on Rayne's face tells me she finds it hard to believe that she and some little vampire kid have anything in common besides evidently sharing a name, but she recovers quickly and bows to Amaya. "Nice to meet you. I'm Rayne. But I guess you already know that."

Amaya giggles in that way that only Japanese schoolgirls can giggle. "Follow me," she instructs. "The others are dying to meet you—" She catches herself and giggles again. "Well, I suppose, to be fair, they are all already dead."

I can't help but giggle back. Vampire humor still cracks me up.

Our little hostess turns and leads us through the small but

tastefully decorated home, done up in minimalist style with low couches and tables, soft lighting, and bamboo screens covering floor-to-ceiling windows. Everything is clean and dainty with no clutter whatsoever. I could never live in a place like this—I feel like I would trash it just by breathing.

We enter a tiny bedroom containing nothing more than a low platform bed, covered in a crimson bedspread. The floor is made up of the same kind of tatami mats the ryokan had, and two red lanterns hang from the ceiling. Amaya walks to the far side of the room and yanks on a string extending from one of the lanterns. A moment later, the bed slides up, into the wall. She pulls aside a mat, revealing a secret trap door, embedded in the floor.

I glance over at Jayden and my sister, who both look equally impressed. Secret passages are so cool.

"Most Japanese homes are built with no basements," Amaya explains as she pulls open the trapdoor, revealing a dark passage below. "But underneath the streets there is an intricate tunnel system, dug out thousands of years ago. Some of them have collapsed, due to earthquakes. And others were incorporated into the subway system. But many have survived and we use them to get around the city during daylight hours." She gestures to the trapdoor. "After you," she says.

I look down into the darkness, not loving what she just said about earthquakes. I've never been a big fan of dark, closed-in spaces, to be honest. It's one of the reasons I'd have made a lousy vampire. The coffin thing would just never fly.

"It's okay," she adds. "It's perfectly safe."

Oh, what the hell. I gingerly take a step down the ladder and into the tunnel below. Once on the ground, my eyes adjust to the dim lighting, made up of a set of little Japanese lanterns strung along the concrete walls. Behind me, Jayden and Rayne follow suit, with Amaya coming in last, pulling the trapdoor shut behind her and pressing a button on the wall, which, I assume, replaces the bed over the trapdoor. Pretty cool, I must admit, though losing the light from above is making the claustrophobia kick in big-time. I shudder and try to get a grip.

"Follow me," Amaya instructs, taking the lead down the underground corridor. My sister falls in line behind her, not a care in the world. I take a furtive glance at the ceiling to judge its stability before taking a few hesitant steps. This is going to be a long, scary trip. I squeeze my eyes shut, then force them open, trying to rouse some courage.

A moment later, I feel a fluttering at my fingers and realize Jayden has reached out to take my hand in his, squeezing it tightly. I look over and catch his sympathetic eyes shining in the darkness. He can tell I'm freaked-out without me even saying so. I squeeze his hand thankfully in return and offer him a small smile, feeling a little better from the camaraderie. Of course, Rayne picks that moment to turn around to locate us and I can see her suspicious glance at our hands. But I shrug her off. After all, there's nothing that says friends can't hold hands, right?

Though, truth be told, friends probably shouldn't intertwine their thumbs together as they weave through the darkness . . .

Finally, after what seems an eternity of dark walking, we reach a metal ladder climbing up into the darkness. Amaya presses another magical button and a trapdoor in the ceiling slides open, letting in very welcome rays of light.

Relieved beyond belief, I rush up the ladder and into what appears to be some kind of dressing room. Dozens of young Japanese vampires are milling about, checking their makeup in mirrors, brushing their long black hair, or straightening their very Gothed-out clothing.

"Now, this is more like it!" Rayne exclaims as she pokes her head up. "Finally a vampire coven with a sense of style." She pops out of the hole and nods her head as she takes in all of the outfits. "I so need to know where you guys shop."

Amaya giggles as she climbs through the trap door and helps Jayden up behind her. "Sorry to disappoint you, Rayne, but those are just their costumes. In real life, they dress much differently." She points to a girl in jean shorts and high heels walking out of the bathroom. "That is more like what they normally wear."

Rayne sighs. She will never find her true Gothy coven, will she?

"Why costumes?" I repeat questioningly.

"The patrons at Bite Club like their vampires to look like vampires," Suki, the girl from the night before, steps up to us and explains with a small smile. "Or at least what they assume vampires should look like. And since they pay good money, we don't like to disappoint them."

"Oh," I realize. "So these are the biters?" I look around at the scurrying teenagers, suddenly feeling like I'm backstage at a strip club or something. I try to remember what Rayne has told me about Blood Bars. "People hire them to suck their blood?"

"Yes, this is one of three licensed Blood Bars in Tokyo," Amaya agrees. "Where vampires are allowed to take blood from humans. The humans pay a lot of money to be drunk from. It feels very good to them."

My first instinct is to recoil in disgust. But then I flash back to the ryokan last night. Jayden's mouth on my neck. The ecstasy of the blood draining from me. The horrible withdrawal feeling when he pulled away. I shudder. Maybe I'm just as bad as the rest of them. Though, of course, I was acting on a noble purpose—trying to save someone's life. They're just here for kicks.

"Do a lot of humans come here?" Jayden asks.

Suki nods. "More than you would think. Businessmen, tourists. Vampire fanatics from around the world. Many countries have made Blood Bars illegal so if you wanted to try it, you'd have to come here."

"You make it sound like a brothel," I say, unable to hide the disgust in my voice.

Amaya shoots me a sharp look. "These workers are honorable vampires. They do not have . . . relations . . . with humans. They serve them dinner and suck their blood. And that is all. The vampires are paid a decent wage for their services. And they are no longer hungry, which cuts down on random blood crime on the streets of Tokyo."

I suppose she's got a point there. But still, I can't help think the whole operation is more than a bit sleazy. Maybe it's the way the vampires are dressed. Or the sultry makeup on their faces. Suddenly this whole thing seems like a bad idea. Jayden, sinking his teeth into some disgusting weird European businessman who's looking to get his rocks off . . .

"Jayden, if you don't want to do this—" I start.

But Rayne cuts me off. "Sunny, can I talk to you for a moment?" she asks. Then adds, "Alone?"

I reluctantly follow her over to an empty corner of the room. She turns to me, her face grave. "Look, you need to chill," she says. "I've done my research on this place. It's all normal and legal and sanctioned by Japanese Slayer Inc. The humans are all blood tested before they are allowed club membership and there are guards inside to make sure nothing gets out of hand." She pauses, then adds, "Don't ruin Jayden's chance for a decent meal because you're jealous of the chick he's going to chow down on."

I hang my head. Am I that obvious? "I'm not—"

"What? Jealous? Do you think I'm an idiot?" Rayne demands. "Please. I see the way you look at that guy. I know you still have feelings for him, even if you won't admit it to yourself. I mean, you were just holding hands, for God's sake!"

"I was afraid of the dark!"

Rayne rolls her eyes. "What would Magnus do if he saw you just now?"

"Magnus can go to hell. He wanted to have Jayden killed."

"You don't know that for sure," Rayne reminds me. "And if he did, I'm sure he had a very good reason." She shakes her head. "And here they say I'm the one with the trust issues."

I gnaw at my lower lip, hating that she's making sense. Since when did my crazy sister become the voice of reason in the family? "Fine," I relent. "Take Jayden into Bite Club. But don't let him leave your sight, okay? We've come all this way. I don't want anything to happen to him."

My sister nods resolutely. "Done and done," she says, reaching over to give me a quick hug. Then we rejoin our group.

"Sunny, I'll show you to the café outside," Amaya says. "You can wait for them there."

Of course I'm not allowed inside. Typical.

"Don't worry, Sun," Rayne adds. "We'll be back before you know it. And Jayden will be feeling a heck of a lot better."

And so we part. Amaya leads me out through a door on the right into a small, cheery café, as promised. After she leaves, I order myself a bubble tea, and try to keep my mind from imagining sweet Jayden morphing into a monster and gulping down a stranger's blood.

It's just dinner, I try to remind myself. *Not sex.*

Not that I should care if it was sex. Jayden isn't my boyfriend. And the more I try to cling to our sort-of half relationship, half friendship, the more unfair it is for him. He should be trying to make new friends, find true love. But every time he makes a move to do so, like with Elizabeth, I end up freaking out like a jealous girlfriend, reeling him back in. Then, every time he does come back to me, telling me he loves me, I push him away.

I need to stop leading him on. To let him go and find his own happiness instead of dragging him down into my misery. I have a boyfriend. Leader of the Blood Coven. Powerful, majestic, beautiful . . .

And, quite possibly, completely untrustworthy.

An hour goes by and I glumly order another tea. How long do these things usually take? I should have asked Amaya.

Suddenly, I see a flash of movement out of the corner of my eyes. Then a high-pitched scream.

"Where is it? Tell us now!" shouts an angry male voice.

I look up, my eyes widening in horror. A group of red-cloaked individuals have just entered the restaurant, armed to the teeth. One of them has my waiter up against the wall, knife to his throat.

Oh my God. The Alphas are here!?

17

Horrified, I duck under the table. Could it really be? The Alphas? Invading the Bite Club? Now, of all times? Is this some kind of massive coincidence? Or did someone from the Cosplay Coven sell us out?

I peek above the table, my heart pounding as the scene unfolds. The Alphas are masked, but I'd recognize those red cloaks anywhere. Not to mention their arrogant swaggers as they surround a helpless waiter who I'm guessing is pleading for his life in a stream of frightened Japanese.

"Where's the door?" demands a familiar-sounding voice. I start, realizing it's Leanna—Corbin's friend and fellow Alpha slayer—one of the core crew back at Riverdale Slay School. She's mixed up in this, too? "Where's the door to this . . . Bite Club?"

The poor waiter continues babbling in Japanese, gesturing wildly with his hands, his eyes bulging from their sockets. To Leanna's right, a shorter, stockier male figure—Peter, I guess— slides a sleek katana from its sheath and raises it to the waiter's throat.

"Does this help jog your memory?" he asks with a sick grin. Geez, when did the Alphas become so bloodthirsty? Back at Riverdale they seemed okay, with the exception of jerky Corbin. And even he was just like your typical bratty bad boy. Not a serial killer going after innocent druids and restaurant employees.

I turn back to the scene. It's probably lucky the waiter is wearing a black suit, because my guess is he's peeing himself right about now. Not that I blame him. I'm semi-safe under a table and I'm still freaking out. At the back end of the café, his coworkers, mostly a group of teen girls, huddle fearfully, probably praying they won't end up next. The rest of the place has completely cleared out.

"Good God, Peter, put that stupid thing away," cuts in a third voice, this one haughty and definitely male. "Let the poor man go. He obviously doesn't know anything."

I watch as a tall, lanky figure strolls over to his friend and shoves him aside with such force that Peter goes sprawling to the ground with a surprised yelp. Yup, vampire Corbin—the gang's all here.

As the waiter dives out of the line of fire, blubbering in relief, Corbin pulls down his hood, revealing a shock of black hair as he starts sniffing the room. I remember Rayne telling me his parents were killed by a vampire at a Blood Bar and wonder if all of this is just his way of getting revenge. Maybe it's nothing to do with the Blood Coven and the Alphas. Maybe he's just on a personal vendetta and we're a lousy coincidence.

Not that any of this will help my sister if he discovers her inside, however. After what she did to him, I'm pretty sure he doesn't consider her his BFF by any means and probably has his stake set to kill. I have to get in there and warn her! But how? They're practically standing right next to the secret door I came through, though they don't know it yet. And the only other entrance I know of is all the way back at that Harajuku house.

"Are you sure we're in the right place, hon?" Leanna asks, putting a gloved hand on Corbin's arm. He shrugs her off.

"Yes, yes, of course we are," he says impatiently. He sniffs the air again, then places a hand on the red-painted wall. Even from my distance, I can see his eyes shining with excitement. "This is it," he announces. "It's behind this false wall."

His three companions walk over to the wall, feeling for the secret door. But Corbin stops them. "Don't waste your time," he instructs. "Just bust it down. Vampires don't deserve the courtesy of knocking."

And so they do, hacking away at the drywall with serious-looking machetes. It doesn't take long for the wall to cave in and red light to spill into the café.

Corbin rips out a particularly large piece of drywall, letting me know for certain that he managed to score superstrength as one of his vampire powers. My sister would be so jealous. "Come on," he says, stepping through the opening. "Let's do this."

The others follow and soon we're Alpha-free again. The waiters and waitresses run toward the front door, whispering to one another in terrified tones. They're the lucky ones and they know it. From beyond the hole in the wall, I can hear the sounds of gunshots, followed by piercing screams.

I slip out of the booth, my whole body shaking like a leaf with fear and indecision. What should I do? Should I call the Blood Coven? But they'd never get here in time! No, it's up to me now. Sunny McDonald—the non-kick-ass twin—to save the day. But what can I do? I don't have Corbin's superstrength, that's for sure. I probably can't even fight a mortal Alpha.

Though . . . I could . . . look like one . . .

Inspiration striking, I close my eyes and concentrate with all my might, visualizing their crimson red cloaks solidly in my mind. And a moment later, thanks to my fairy powers, I'm wearing one. Along with a mask, just like their own. Of course, I'm sadly not able to conjure up any actual weapons, but since I wouldn't know the first thing about how to use them, even if I did, I guess it's for the best anyway.

I leap out of the booth and into the hole in the wall, ready to face whatever's on the other side. It takes my eyes a minute to adjust to the darkness, and once they do, I kind of wish they hadn't. The place is a disaster area. A complete massacre of epic proportions. Everywhere I look, mortals lie bleeding on the ground, pleading for their lives, while clouds of dust from staked vampires waft through the air. I accidentally breathe some in through my nose and immediately start choking, praying this isn't all that's left of my sister or Jayden.

But I don't panic; instead, I force myself to take a deep breath before gingerly making my way down the hallway and into the changing room we started in. What once was a room full of giggling teens is now just a big pile of dust. My stomach roils and it's all I can do not to throw up. I try to tell myself that I'd know, somehow, if my sister were dead—twin intuition and all that—

but somehow I'm not so sure. And what about Jayden? My heart lurches as I imagine never being able to talk to him again.

A bright spotlight suddenly shines into the room and I leap back in surprise. A lone figure in a short skirt and big boots is silhouetted in the doorway, gripping a knife in her hands.

"Prepare to die," she spits, before she lunges at me.

18

"Wait! Rayne! It's me! Sunny!" I cry as my sister dives on top of me, ready to strike. I fumble at my hood, thankful I didn't go for a full metamorphosis this time around. She shines her light down at my face, blinding me for a moment.

"Sunny?" she cries, her voice thankfully full of recognition. "What are you doing in here? And why are you wearing one of their cloaks?"

"I'm trying to rescue you, you dummy."

She rolls off of me and scrambles to her feet. "I don't need rescuing," she replies cockily. Then she catches my expression and smiles. "Though, of course, I do appreciate the effort."

I brush the dust off my clothes, trying not to remind myself they came from a vaporized vampire's skin. "What about Jayden?" I ask, my heart in my throat as I await her answer.

"He's hiding in Bite Room C," she informs me. "Don't worry,

I made sure he was safe, just as I promised I would. I had no idea we were in for such a massacre of epic proportion when I made that promise or I might have asked for hazard pay."

"It was Corbin," I inform her. "Him and the rest of the Alphas. They came in through the café." My voice breaks. "I thought they were going to kill you."

"I'm not that easy to kill," Rayne scoffs in her regular tough-girl way, but, at the same time, I can tell she's visibly shaken by the idea that Corbin's behind all of this. "I wonder how he found us," she muses.

"It seems like wherever we go, they're one step ahead of us," I say. "First the Holy Grail. Now the Blood Bar . . ."

Rayne sheaths her knife and brings out her stake. "Go find Jayden," she instructs. "I'm going to go have a little talk with Corbin and see what's up. And by talk, I mean, I'm going to stake that bastard through the heart if he gives me half the chance."

"I'm sure he's thinking the same thing about you."

"Probably. But I'm better than him," she says with a smirk. Then she sobers. "Sunny, give me a little credit here. I'm not going to go out, stakes blazing. I'm just going to do a little recon is all. The Consortium needs to know what the Alphas are up to." She pauses, then adds, "Why don't you go find Jayden, get him out of here, and meet me back at the ryokan? We'll regroup and figure out our next strategy there."

"Fine," I reply, knowing it will do no good to argue with my headstrong sister. "I'll see you in about an hour."

My sister nods and turns to run out of the room. "Rayne!" I call back to her. She stops and turns around, her face impatient.

"Yeah?"

"Be safe, okay?" I say, giving her my best pleading look. "For my sake, if not your own."

"Always, little sister," she teases, before disappearing into the night. I watch her go, then head off to try to find Bite Room C and Jayden, trying to shake the bad feeling I have about all of this.

Jayden is mostly silent on the way back to the ryokan, as if still shell-shocked over the night's events. Not that I blame him. When I found him in Bite Room C, he was almost catatonic with fear. It took a lot of reassuring to get him to leave his hiding spot and follow me out of the Blood Bar.

Once we get inside our cozy little room, I pull out the futon mats and help him down onto one of them, covering him with a thick comforter. But he's still shaking like crazy, so eventually I decide to lie down next to him, pulling him toward my own body to share my mortal warmth. He's like an ice cube, even for a cold-blooded vampire, as he cuddles against me.

"They killed everyone," he whispers, his mouth against my ear. "It was so awful. All these vampires—just exploding into oblivion. And those people . . . those innocent people . . ." He shakes his head, remembering. "I tried to get the girl I was drinking from to come with me to hide. But she only wanted to escape." He shudders. "I heard her down the hall . . . screaming and screaming . . . and then . . . nothing."

My heart aches for him; I can't imagine what it must be like to witness such carnage. "I'm so glad you're okay," I murmur, rocking him close to me. "I was so scared that you'd been killed, too."

"I'm alive 'cause I hid like a coward," he spits out ruefully. "Let everyone else die around me instead."

I pull away, giving him a sharp look. "What could you have done? You would have just gotten yourself killed if you tried to play hero."

"What about you? You risked your life going in there."

"I had a disguise," I remind him. "And besides, I had to make up for you saving my life back in Vegas. Now we're even."

"Actually I think you might be a little ahead at this point."

We fall back into our embrace and I can feel his heart beating wildly against my own. It's hard to believe just a short time ago we were fighting for our lives. Now I feel so warm and safe and cozy in our tiny room. Me and Jayden, against the world.

"Oh, Sunny," he murmurs, evidently sharing my sentiments. He nuzzles his head against my shoulder. "I'm so sorry. I've been acting like such a jerk to you this whole trip."

I reach out to smooth his razor-cut black hair. "It's okay," I assure him. "You've been going through a lot. It's understandable."

"It's not that, though," he insists. "I mean, yeah, the vampire thing is stressful and all. But that's not why I've been so mad at you."

I prop my head on my elbow to study him questioningly. "You're mad at me?"

He sighs, rolling over onto his back to stare up at the ceiling. "Well, no. I mean, I think I'm mostly mad at myself, I guess. I just . . ." He lets out a long, frustrated sigh. "I can't believe I'm going to say this," he mutters, half to himself.

"Say what, Jayden?" I press, my heart pounding in my chest as I wonder if I truly want to know.

At first I think he's not going to speak. But finally he opens his mouth. "I was lying there, hiding under the bed in the Bite Club, pretty sure I was going to die. And I kept thinking, *I'm going to die and I'm never going to get a chance to tell Sunny how much she means to me."* His voice cracks on the last sentence and I can see the tears welling up in his eyes.

"Oh, Jayden," I murmur, reaching out to him. But he grabs my hand and pushes it away.

"Let me finish," he begs, "or I'll lose my nerve again." He laughs bitterly, then he turns to face me, reaching out and cupping my chin with his hand, steering my face to his so our eyes are locked onto one another. A chill trips down my spine and I hold my breath, trying desperately to ready myself for his impending words.

"Sunny, I love you," he says simply. "I've loved you since the first moment I saw you walk into the Sun Casino in Vegas. I've been trying to be good—to hold back and keep it inside—telling myself that I don't want to make things harder for you by burdening you with these feelings. After all, you made your choice. You chose Magnus and I let you walk away." He shakes his head, the tears tumbling from his eyes. "God, that was the stupidest thing I've ever done. Giving you back to him—who doesn't even deserve you."

I struggle to draw in a breath, my heart breaking at his raw, honest words. I remember that day—in the hospital room when I tried to give my heart to Jayden. And he told me to go back to Magnus and try to work things out. It had all seemed so noble and selfless of him at the time. But had it been the right thing for me to do?

Since then, I've been working so hard at my relationship with Magnus. Trying to get over the trust issues we have and always wondering where his loyalties truly lie. Fighting over stupid things—trying and failing to fit into his world while he tried and failed to fit into mine.

With Jayden, it's so easy. We're like two twin souls, with the same desires and dreams. Like two children coming together, finding each other and bonding together against the cold, hard world. With Jayden, I never have to doubt his motives. I never have to wonder if he's lying to me. He's simple and open and pure and good and everything I always dreamed about in a boyfriend.

And he loves me. With all his heart. He's already proven he'd gladly die for me. And there's no conflict of a stupid coven to get in his way.

"Sorry," he says, his face pinkening into a small blush. "Again, I don't mean to make things difficult for you. I just can't keep going, pretending you don't mean everything to me." He gives a sad little laugh. "So now you know. And you can choose to walk away again—and I won't stop you. Or you can give yourself to me and let me love you the way you deserve to be loved. Dedicating my entire life—mortal or vampire—to making you happy."

He stops and looks at me with his big puppy-dog eyes and I find I can't speak, my throat is so clogged with tears. And so I do the only thing I know how. I kiss him. Our mouths tumbling over each other in desperate abandon—not thinking, not analyzing, not wondering what the consequences might be to something like this. Just kissing and loving and worshiping each other. The salty taste of our tears mixing with the sweetest ecstasy. A perfect dream bubble in a nightmare of a world.

It's Jayden who pulls away first. "I'm sorry," he says, a bashful expression on his face. "I shouldn't have . . ."

I put a finger to his lips—swollen and bruised from my mouth. "It's okay," I assure him. "I . . . I wanted to."

He looks at me with a shy smile. "Yeah?" he asks, his voice so full of hope it breaks my heart all over again. A part of me wildly demands to know what the hell I think I'm doing, but I push it deep down inside. There will be time for overanalysis later.

"Jayden. I have feelings for you," I admit. "I always have, as much as I've tried to hide them for your own good. I didn't want to hurt you. Or let you down if I couldn't follow through. I've already caused you enough pain." I draw in a breath. "But I do love you. I love you so much, Jayden, and I'm sick of trying to deny it to myself."

"What about Magnus?" he asks softly, breathing the name I'm trying to block out of my mind.

I roll onto my back, staring up at the ceiling. "I don't know," I say with a sigh. "After how we left things back in England, I don't even know where we stand right now. I mean, of course I love him. But I don't know if I can trust him. And I don't want a relationship based on lies." I roll back over to face Jayden. "I mean, look at you. You're so open and honest. I know I can trust you with my heart and soul. And I need that. I really need that."

I lean forward to kiss him again, desperate to feel his lips brush against mine one more time. But instead, he stops me, pressing a hand to my chest.

"Wait," he says, his eyes dropping to the floor.

I look at him, puzzled. "What?" I ask, taking in his distraught expression. "What's wrong?"

"I need to tell you something." He rakes a hand through his black hair. "You say I'm honest, but I haven't been entirely truthful to you."

Fear trips down my spine at his words. "What are you saying?" I manage to spit out.

"I . . ." Jayden swallows hard. "Oh God. Promise you won't hate me, Sun. I couldn't bear to have you hate me."

Now the fear is in my gut, twisting like a knife. "What, Jayden?"

I ask, gritting my teeth in an attempt to keep my composure. "Tell me. Now."

"I . . . well, I didn't tell you the exact truth. About the whole vampire thing, I mean."

"You mean Cornelius biting you?"

"I mean that he didn't bite me. I was fine after that whole encounter," Jayden confesses. "But then you disappeared and I started getting really depressed. And . . . angry, I guess. Angry that you chose someone else. A bloodsucker—a living corpse— over me. I thought . . ." He shrugs. "I thought maybe if I found a way to become a vampire I'd be more appealing to you. That maybe you'd leave Magnus and be mine."

"But that's crazy! Why would you—?"

"I don't know!" Jayden interrupts fiercely. "I told you, I wasn't thinking straight. I was so depressed and angry and . . . I don't know. In any case, I headed down to the vampire bar that I knew Cornelius used to frequent. And I started propositioning vampires, asking them to turn me. My plan was to get one of them to do the job, then take the first plane back to Massachusetts— where I thought you were—and profess my love."

"But no vampire would do that. It's completely against protocol. You have to be certified first! And go through the training."

He nods. "I found that out pretty quick. Everyone turned me down. Except for one vampire." He looks up at me, his eyes brimming with blood tears. "His name was Corbin. He wore a red cloak."

I almost fall off my chair. "Oh my God."

"He and the other Alphas burst into the bar on a mission of vengeance, killing every vampire and human in sight, just as they did today. I begged him to spare my life—telling him I knew you and Magnus and the Blood Coven—thinking maybe it would help my case. He got this weird gleam in his eyes and asked me if I wanted to become a vampire."

"So Corbin turned you," I say dully. "And let me guess, he can hear your thoughts now. That's how they've been able to stay one step ahead of us. To steal the Grail. To break into the Bite Club."

Jayden cringes. "Probably," he says. "I don't know. Whatever he did to me . . . well, he didn't finish. He got interrupted halfway through the process by a vampire mob, which chased him off. Which I guess is why I only turned half vamp. Too sick to follow through with my plan to go find you. I couldn't believe it when you found me instead. It was like a dream wrapped in a nightmare."

"Oh, Jayden," I cry, my heart breaking. "Why? Why would you do such a thing?"

"Because I wanted you to love me," he says simply, his voice hoarse with pain. "I wanted to be the kind of guy you respected."

I rise to my feet, anger churning in my gut. I can't believe it. Lied to again. Is no man alive worth my trust?

"And now, instead, you're a monster who's put the entire vampire race in danger."

"I don't care about the vampire race," he moans. "I only care about you."

I shake my head. There's no use arguing. "I've got to go," I tell him. "I've got to warn the coven."

"I'll come with you!"

"Absolutely not! You've done enough already." I squeeze my hands into fists. "God, I should have never taken you away from England in the first place. Magnus was right. Damn it, he was right all along!" Why hadn't I trusted him? Why had I just assumed he wasn't looking out for my best interests?

"What am I supposed to do?" Jayden asks, his eyes wide and frightened.

"I don't know. Stake yourself in the heart for all I care," I growl.

He looks at me with his big green eyes, his face a study of torment and regret. "I'm so sorry, Sunny," he murmurs. "I never meant—"

I catch his expression and part of me melts. Part of me wants nothing more than to take him into my arms and hug him and say I understand and forgive him because he did it for me. He did it to win my love. How can I blame him for something so innocent and pure?

But I have to. I have to stay strong. It will do no good to be soft on him now. Doing so will only endanger the lives of thousands.

Suddenly I get a real idea of the kinds of decisions I've been asking Magnus to make.

"Look, I'm sorry," I say. "I didn't mean the whole stake thing. But you gotta stay here, okay? When Rayne shows up, let her know what's going on and have her call me ASAP."

"I will," he says, staring down at the floor. "Sunny, I'm really sorry."

I shake my head as I walk out of the room. "I know you are. But it doesn't do me much good now."

19

"Yes, hi, I'm looking for a guest named Magnus?" I inform the hotel clerk at the Park Hyatt hotel in Shinjuku about an hour later. I thought taking a cab would save me time, but traffic was so terrible, it took twice as long. And gave me way too much time to think about what just happened.

I can't believe I actually opened up to Jayden. Gave him my trust. Admitted my love. Only to find out he's just as bad as the rest of them. A liar. Just like my dad. Just like Magnus. Will I ever meet a guy who will just respect me enough to tell me the freaking truth? God! I can't believe I trusted Jayden. That I came all the way to Japan to try to save his life—putting everyone I love—and myself—in danger. Blaming myself, thinking I was responsible for his predicament. But no. The idiot did it all to himself. Willingly turned himself into an undead monster, just so he could hook up with me. And, sure, that might sound kind of romantic except for the fact that he then just sat back and let me beat myself up about the whole thing—believing that it was all my fault the poor guy pretty much lost his soul.

I can't believe I actually felt sorry for him. I can't believe I kissed him. I'm so ashamed of myself.

"Magnus?" the clerk repeats. "No one here by that name. So sorry."

I bite my lower lip. Of course there isn't. They're here under-cover to spy on the Alphas. They're probably using pseudonyms. "Maybe you've seen him?" I ask the clerk without much hope. "He's about this tall? Kind of looks like Orlando Bloom in *Pirates of the Caribbean*? Green eyes to die for?"

The clerk just stares at me. "So sorry," he repeats.

Great. I walk over to a nearby bench and plop down. Here I am, just waiting to confess my sins, and I can't even find my boy-friend to do it. And seeing as this hotel is at least fifty floors high with nearly two hundred guest rooms, the chances of me finding him on my own are slim to none.

I try dialing his cell phone again, but it goes right to voice mail. He's probably in a meeting, as usual. I try my sister, too, but when the call is picked up, it's not Rayne on the other end. In-stead, a high-pitched voice says something I can't understand in Japanese.

"Is Rayne there?" I try. "Rayne McDonald?" A gnawing worry starts eating at my stomach. Why would someone else answer her phone? Is she in trouble? "Do you speak English?"

"Ah, English. Yes," says the voice on the other end. "I found phone. In alley. You know owner?"

Oh God. I white-knuckle my mobile, fear now washing over me in a wave. Maybe she just dropped it by mistake. No big deal. She's already over at the ryokan, just waiting for me.

I hope . . .

I try to get more details—what alley, what neighborhood, was it near the Bite Club? But the woman's halting English doesn't give me much to work with. Finally I give up, hanging up the phone and pacing the lobby, wondering what I should do. Magnus needs to know what's going on so he can alert the Consortium. But at the same time, I can't just hang around here when my sister could be in serious trouble.

Rayne, why did you have to go play the hero?

Just as I'm about to give up and head back and look for my sister, I catch movement out of the corner of my eye. I look up to watch the elevator doors slide open. My eyes widen as I recognize the tall blond woman in a crisp blue suit stroll into the lobby. Marcia. Magnus's annoying *Brady Bunch*–esque secretary! I've never been so happy to see the bitch in all my life!

"Marcia!" I cry, scrambling up from my seat. "Oh my God, I need to find Magnus. Can you tell me what room he's in?"

The vampire arches a cool eyebrow. "Well, well," she sniffs. "Look what the bats dragged in. Aren't you supposed to be on some holiday in jolly old England or something?" She looks a little too pleased with herself as she asks. Probably imagining all the trouble I'm going to get in with her boss when he finds out I'm here.

But I don't have time to indulge her fantasies at the moment. "Come on, M," I plead. "You can belittle me later, I promise. But I have to find Magnus now. I've got something really important to tell him."

"Lord Magnus is in meetings all night with the other members of the Consortium," Marcia informs me haughtily. "He asked not to be disturbed. Now, if you'll excuse me . . ." She pushes by, hip-checking me on purpose, I'm sure of it. She's still in love with Magnus and hates the fact that he picked a mortal chick over her illustrious vampiric secretarial self.

"Come on, Marcia," I beg. "This is important."

Marcia lets out a long, drawn-out sigh. "Whatever you have to say to Lord Magnus, you can tell me and I'll try to relay it to him between meetings. But no promises."

Argh. As if I'd trust her. "Come on," I beg. "This is an emergency! Don't be like this."

She cocks her head at me, her eyes burning with self-righteous fire. "Don't be like what?" she demands. Uh-oh. "Don't be a good assistant with the coven's best interests at heart?" She scowls. "Why are you even here, anyway? You'll only distract him again. Trying to pull him away from his important duties to our coven with your little whiny 'What about me?' shtick."

I stare at her, horrified, wanting to defend myself, but not sure where to begin.

"You know, we could have already defeated the Alphas if Lord Magnus hadn't skipped out to rescue you in Fairyland," she continues. "And then, when he's already on thin ice with the Consortium, he completely disobeys their orders and jaunts over to England with you, because you batted your eyelashes and pleaded." She squeezes her hands into fists, her manicured nails digging into her palms. "And now you're back. And with more trouble, I'm sure. I beg of you: Go home. Leave Magnus alone. We need him too much in this war to have him distracted over and over again by your pretty face."

My shoulders slump at her words. Is that really what they all think of me? That I'm just this human, getting in the way of important vampire business? That Magnus is weak for taking my side? Here I've been blaming him for putting the Blood Coven before me, when all along his own people think he's putting me before the Blood Coven.

The poor guy can't win.

"Look," I try. "I know I've been a selfish bitch in the past. And you have no reason to like me, I get it. But Marcia, what I've found out about the Alphas—it could put the Consortium at risk. And I need to tell Magnus ASAP. The entire vampire race could be in danger."

She narrows her eyes and for a moment, she doesn't speak. Finally she nods. "Okay," she says with resignation. "I'll see what I can do. But you'd better not be bluffing."

"I wish I were."

"Stay here. I'll go interrupt his meeting."

I collapse onto the sleek white leather bench, biting my nails as I wait to see if Magnus will come down. Trying to prepare myself for his inevitable wrath. Because, let's face it, he's so not going to be pleased with what I have to say. In fact, when this is all over, I wonder if he'll even talk to me again. I wouldn't blame him, I suppose, if he didn't.

I'm not sure, to be honest, I'd talk to myself.

20

About ten minutes later, the elevator doors slide open once again and Magnus steps out, scanning the room. I rise to my feet just as his eyes fall upon me.

"I guess I shouldn't be surprised," he says stiffly. "You never do manage to follow orders."

I hang my head. "I'm sorry."

I wait for his anger, his screams of condemnation. But they don't come. Instead he asks, "So, to what do I owe this . . . honor?"

Where to even begin? I shuffle from foot to foot. "Can we talk somewhere private?"

He nods. "Come upstairs to my hotel room."

I follow him back onto the elevator and we shoot up into the sky. A few minutes later we step into one of the most luxurious hotel rooms I've ever seen. With a view fifty-something stories up looking down on the neon wonderland they call Shinjuku.

"Wow," I say, walking over to the floor-to-ceiling window. "Rayne told me these were sweet digs. But I had no idea—"

"So your sister is in on this little escapade as well," Magnus says grimly, sitting down on the bed. "Of course."

I turn back to face him. Here goes nothing. "Turns out Jayden wasn't bitten by Cornelius after all," I admit. "He was bitten by Corbin. And now the two of them share some kind of psychic link. That's why the Alphas were able to locate the Holy Grail. I told Jayden where it was. And that's why they raided the Bite Club in Harajuku."

Magnus squeezes his eyes shut, then opens them again. "What else?" he asks in a tight voice.

I kick the carpet with my foot. "They probably know that you're here."

"Here, in Japan?"

"Here in the Park Hyatt. Rayne was going off about how awesome it was. I'm sure Jayden heard her."

"Oh, Sunny." My boyfriend sighs deeply. "Why couldn't you have just trusted me and stayed in England as I asked?"

I frown. "Um, so I could just let you murder Jayden? I don't think so. I mean, I know he lied—and believe me, I'm furious with him, too. But that doesn't mean he deserves to die."

Magnus stares at me, a puzzled look on his face. "What are you talking about?"

"I overheard Tanner talking to Lucedio. You ordered him to poison Jayden and make it look like his body didn't accept the transfusion."

Magnus rises to his feet. "I don't know what you think you heard," he replies bitterly. "But I can assure you, I ordered no such thing."

"But—"

"You really will trust anyone in the world—even vampires you barely know—over your own boyfriend, won't you?" Magnus growls, pacing the room. "I don't even know what to say about that."

I hang my head in shame. Was it true? Did he really know nothing about this? "I'm sorry," I say, though the words seem so useless. "I just . . . I heard it and I freaked out. And I had to get Jayden out of there."

"And so you brought him here. And put us all in danger."

"Well, to be fair, I didn't know about the Corbin thing. I just found that out right before I came here to see you. He finally admitted it to me."

"Well, isn't that bloody noble of him."

I rise to my feet, looking pleadingly at Magnus. "I screwed up," I admit. "I know it. And I don't deserve your forgiveness. But I need your help."

He rakes a hand through his hair, freeing it from its ponytail. "Of course," he says, his voice laced with sarcasm. "How can I be of assistance?"

"It's Rayne. After the Alphas attacked at Bite Club, she went after Corbin. And I haven't heard from her since. I tried calling her cell, but the woman who answered said she found it discarded in an alleyway. I'm worried."

Magnus whirls around, his eyes wide and frightened. "She went after them? Alone—without backup? Is she crazy?"

"Um, we're talking about Rayne here, remember?"

"Hell," he swears, stalking over to the hotel phone and picking up the receiver. He presses a few buttons. "Jareth?" he says, after a moment. "Have you heard from Rayne?" He waits for a reply. "Okay," he says. "Well, let me know if she reports in. Yes, I'll tell you the whole story. It's probably nothing but . . ." He pauses.

"Yes, yes, I promise. I've got to go." He hangs up the phone and sinks back onto the bed, scrubbing his face with his hands. "Pyrus is going to kill me."

"Who cares about him?" I demand. "My sister could be in trouble!"

"Ah, yes, once again, this is all about you," Magnus notes. "Who cares that Rayne put herself in trouble by not following orders? And who cares that I'm going to be the one to pay if the Alphas have really taken her." He squeezes his hands into fists. "Rayne knew full well she was supposed to stay here, under the protection of the Blood Coven. She knew the Alphas would stop at nothing to kidnap her and harvest her blood. And yet, she—just like her sister—decided to defy those orders and sneak out on some crazy mission she felt was more important. Putting all of vampire kind in danger."

He turns to me, his eyes bloodshot and wild. "You think *I'm* the one who's not trustworthy?" he demands. "You think *my* loyalties are divided? You don't care one bit about what I go through on a daily basis. Or how much trouble I'm constantly in for siding with you instead of my bosses. And if I even hint that I have a duty to perform that doesn't directly benefit you, you automatically start questioning my loyalty or making up crazy things in your head that I'm somehow lying to you and working behind your back to murder your friends."

I stare at him, unable to speak. Oh God, have I really been so selfish?

"I'm not saying the Consortium is perfect," he continues. "But it's the only government we've got. And when I took command as Master of the Blood Coven, I made a vow to uphold their laws, no matter what. In exchange, my vampires get protection and peace," he explains. "I've seen what happens to covens tossed out of the Consortium for not obeying their rules. They lose everything. They live in squalor—in fear for their lives. There's never enough blood . . ." He frowns. "I can't let that happen to my people."

He rises from the bed and walks over to the window, crossing his arms over his chest and staring out into the night sky. I let out a frustrated breath, feeling the tears well up into my eyes as my mind races over the events of the last few days. Here I've been thinking I'm the noble heroine, on a mission to save a life. But am I really the selfish villainess, putting everyone in danger, just as Jayden did?

I glance over at my boyfriend's rigid back. You can practically see the anger coming off him in waves. My heart lurches in my chest and I feel like I'm going to throw up. How am I ever going to get him to forgive me?

I rise slowly to my feet and walk over to him, wrapping myself around him and laying my head on his back. At first I wonder if he's going to shrug me off, push me away. But he just stands there, staring out the window. Not submitting, but not rejecting either. I guess that's something.

"I don't even know what to say," I whisper. "Sorry seems so useless."

At first he doesn't respond. Then he turns slowly, pulling me into an embrace. I collapse against him in relief, feeling the sobs choke my throat at this suggestion of forgiveness. Maybe there's still hope. Maybe I haven't ruined everything . . .

"I'm sorry, too," he whispers. "I know I'm not always forthcoming about the big picture. I try to keep you out of things in an attempt to protect you. But that only makes you worry and doubt me." He pauses, then adds, "And you're not selfish. You're just all heart. You can't stand to see the people you love suffer."

He strokes my head with a gentle hand. "We're a lot alike in that way. I'm protective of my vampires just as you're protective of your sister and friends." He sighs. "It's heartbreaking to see those two good things constantly at odds."

"We need to start working together," I murmur against his chest. "We're stronger together than apart."

He pulls away to look down at me with loving eyes. "I agree," he says with a small smile. "So let's go talk to the Consortium about what's going on here. Together."

I cock my head in question. "What? But I thought mortals weren't allowed in their sessions."

"They're not." He shrugs. "But I don't care anymore. You're my partner. My equal. And it's time I start treating you as such."

"Thank you," I say sincerely. "That means a lot."

"*You* mean a lot," he replies, leaning down to kiss me softly on the head. "Now let's go save your sister."

21

And that's how, an hour later, I find myself the only living girl in a room full of undead. All the premiere voting members of the Vampire Consortium—masters from all over the world—assembled together in a large arena, which, during normal business hours, houses sumo wrestling matches. (And has the stench of sweaty fat guys to prove it.) When the infamous House Speaker, Pyrus, a tuxedoed, bleach-blond vampire who bears a striking resemblance to Gerard from My Chemical Romance, calls on us, Magnus leads me up to the podium at the center of the arena.

"This is Sunshine McDonald," he announces to the crowd. "Royal daughter of Queen Shrinking Violet of the Light Court of Tír na nÓg."

The crowd quiets and I can feel a hundred pairs of eyes focus on me expectantly, and I'm suddenly glad of my fae heritage. At least that gives me a tiny dash of otherworld street cred here. I wonder if I should mention I was actually a vampire for about six days last spring. Would that help or hurt my case?

I step up to the podium with legs that feel like Jell-O. "Um, hello," I try to say into the microphone. But in my nervousness I've leaned in too far, spoken too loud, or just got my iPhone too close to the speaker, and high-pitched feedback screeches across the room. I leap back in surprise, my face heating in embarrassment. *Way to make a professional first impression, Sun.*

I can hear several vampires titter amongst themselves. Jerks. You'd think living a thousand years would give them a more refined sense of humor.

I glance longingly at the exit. Maybe this wasn't such a good idea. Then I feel a presence beside me. Magnus has stepped next to me, strong shouldered and supportive. He squeezes my hand encouragingly. "It's okay," he whispers. "Go on."

Empowered, I step up to the mic a second time, this time keeping my distance. "Hello," I say again, hating the fact that my voice sounds so squeaky and young, as it always does when I'm freaking out. "My name is Sunshine McDonald and I'm here to ask for your help."

I've got their attention now so I draw in a breath and force myself to continue. "My sister is a vampire—a member of the Blood Coven. And she's missing. We have reason to believe she was taken by Alpha operatives who, tonight, raided the Tokyo Bite Club and killed everyone inside."

I wait for the shocked faces, the gasps of horror, the fierce shouts, demanding action, justice, and revenge. We must mobilize. We must track them down. We must get Rayne back.

But, evidently not so much.

"Dude, did you just yawn?" I demand to the Gothy-looking vampire in the front row.

He rolls his kohl-lined eyes. "I'm sorry, who are you again?" he sniffs. "And why are you bothering us with this trivial matter? Are you not aware we're at war here? We don't have time to stage a rescue for every stupid vampire who puts herself in a foolish situation."

I stare at him in shock. Is he for real? Then I realize pretty much everyone in the crowd is nodding their heads in agreement.

"But she's one of you! A member of the Blood Coven!" I protest. "Doesn't that entitle her to some kind of protection? I thought that was what this whole stupid Consortium thing was all about."

"Sunny . . ." Magnus growls low at my side.

"Typical Blood Coven," sneers a buxom, black-haired vampire girl in the back row. "Such do-gooders. They should have named you the Bleeding Heart Coven."

I open my mouth to retort, but Pyrus cuts me off. "What are you really asking for here?" he demands of me. "You want us to stop our delicate negotiations with the Alphas and just go in, fangs blazing, to save some inconsequential vampire who disobeyed orders to stay in the compound and got herself kidnapped because of it?"

I hang my head. It doesn't sound good when he puts it that way. I glance over at Magnus with pleading eyes, begging him to step in. I know I said I wanted to be a part of this, but I didn't know that meant throwing myself to the wolves. I'm beginning to see why Consortium business stresses him out so much.

He gives me a regretful smile, like, *I told you so*, but in a nice way, and gestures for me to step aside. I do so willingly and he takes the microphone out of its holder. "Fellow Consortium members," he addresses the crowd. "Lord Pyrus," he adds, giving a short bow to Mr. Speaker. "I am afraid the missing vampire in question is not so inconsequential after all. You may be familiar with Rayne McDonald, our resident vampiric fae? This is the sister that Sunshine speaks of."

Oh, right. I flush. I should have mentioned her name. I forgot that she's some kind of special case to them. Sure enough, as soon as Magnus says it, the room erupts with excited chatter. Now they're worried. Well, whatever works, I guess.

Pyrus bangs his gavel against the wood block. "I will have order!" he demands and a moment later the talking dies out. He turns to Magnus, his expression grim. I can see my boyfriend gripping the microphone so tightly I'm afraid he's going to crush it with his bare hands.

"How could you have let this happen?" the speaker seethes. "Rayne McDonald was ordered to be under strict guard by your coven the entire trip. You know how valuable she is to us. And you said you'd take care of it."

Magnus grits his teeth. "Rayne can be very . . . determined," he spits out. "I will find out what happened, of course. But I have little doubt of her ability to outsmart my guards, if given the motivation to do so."

"Then you should have chained her up."

"She's a member of my coven, not a prisoner!"

Pyrus shakes his head in disgust. "I should have never trusted your pathetic coven. Now you've ruined everything."

Confusion washes over Magnus's face. "Everything?" he repeats. "I know we had her on retainer but why—"

"How are we going to make a deal with the Alphas now?" Pyrus demands. "Now that we no longer have anything of value to them?"

"Wait, what?" I demand, grabbing the mic from Magnus. "You were planning to trade my sister? To the Alphas?" I turn to

Magnus, fury raging inside of me. Did he know of this? But then I catch the horrified look on his face and I realize there's no way. Magnus may be loyal to his vampires, but he'd never sacrifice my sister—and the blood mate of his best friend—for any political purpose.

And suddenly, I realize I trust that—I trust him—completely and utterly without a speck of doubt.

Magnus pries the microphone back from me and turns to Pyrus. "Could you please enlighten me on this so-called trade?" he asks, his voice tight and anxious. "I do not believe I was made aware of it."

Pyrus sniffs. "It's simple, really. The Alphas informed me that if I were to hand over Rayne McDonald, they would sign a peace treaty with the Consortium. We would transfer our contract from the main Slayer Inc. parent group and use the Alphas from this point forward." He shrugs. "It seemed like a good solution. They'll create their vampiric fae army and use it to protect us."

"Or go back on their word and destroy us," Magnus points out. "How can you trust an organization like that?"

"I don't," the speaker says simply. "But this would have bought us time, at the very least."

"Time bought at the cost of one of my own," Magnus growls, baring his fangs. He looks so scary and fierce—I don't know whether to be proud or frightened. "I should have been consulted. I would never have agreed to something like this!"

"Then you should have been here," Pyrus bites back. "This is war, Magnus. I couldn't sit around twiddling my thumbs, while you were off in England, trying to save some mutant stray."

So that's it. I asked Magnus to abandon his duties to the Consortium, and by doing so, I basically signed my sister's death warrant. I should have listened to him from the start. Trusted his judgment in doing the right thing. Seen the bigger picture here instead of always looking at my own selfish whims. We chose Jayden—who lied and put us all at risk. And in doing so, we doomed my sister.

"In any case, it makes no difference now," Pyrus adds. "Seeing as they've gotten her on their own and now there's nothing we can do about it." He shakes his head. "And no bargaining means war." He turns to the Consortium. "Masters, assemble your armies," he instructs. "Our time is up. Tomorrow evening, we will mobilize against the Alphas. We will bring them down!"

The crowd cheers—caught up in the excitement—and the vampires start scrambling up from their seats. Magnus turns to me, a devastated expression on his face. "I'm sorry," he whispers, in a voice that breaks my heart.

"No, I'm sorry," I whisper back. "I should have never doubted you."

"So that's it then?" Magnus demands of Pyrus as the audience dwindles. "No discussion, no vote? They all just do what you say now, without question?"

Pyrus gives him a self-satisfied smirk. "They know I have their best interests at heart."

"The only thing you have in your poor excuse for a heart is a thirst for power," Magnus snarls. "The Consortium I joined was supposed to be a democracy. And yet suddenly it smells suspiciously of a dictatorship—"

"Lord Magnus, you are out of order," Pyrus interrupts. "If you would like to make a procedural complaint, you can do so tomorrow night by filling out the correct form in triplicate and filing it at the proper—"

"What, so you can bury it in your bureaucracy and keep doing exactly what it is you want to do?" Magnus demands. "Knowing that everyone's too scared to speak up and voice an opinion, fearing that you'll kick them out of the Consortium if they do?" He scowls. "Well, I for one am done with it. The Blood Coven will not go along with your plan until it's been discussed and brought to a vote—as we all vowed to do when we first joined the organization."

Pyrus smirks. "I'm afraid that's no longer your call. By the powers vested in me as Speaker of the Consortium, I hereby remove you from your position as Master of the Blood Coven."

I gasp. Can he do that?

Magnus's face turns stark white. I guess he can.

"And what will happen to my coven?" he asks in a steely voice. As always, he's thinking of his people before himself.

"Your co-master, Jareth, will be placed in command. Hopefully he will prove more loyal to the Consortium than his predecessor."

"That's not fair!" I cry, horrified. But Magnus silences me with a fierce look. I reluctantly snap my mouth closed.

The speaker smiles smugly. "Actually, I think I'm being more than fair. After all, I'm sure Magnus here doesn't want the entire Blood Coven to be punished for his crimes, now, does he?"

Magnus hangs his head. God, this is so not good!

"Take your punishment like a good little vampire, and maybe I will see fit to let you live," Pyrus adds. "But if you lift even one finger to interfere with Consortium business and the upcoming Alpha attack, I will have you staked into oblivion." He smirks. "And you know full well there's not one vampire here who will stop me."

And with that lovely sentiment, he sweeps out of the room,

leaving Magnus and me standing in an empty arena. My boy-friend sinks down onto a nearby bench, his whole body shaking with anger. I run to his side, wondering what I should do, what I should say. It's not often I see him looking lost—so out of control. I feel terrible that I am the one who caused so much of this pain.

"I'm so sorry," I say, feeling the tears well up into my eyes. "I'm so, so sorry. This is all my fault."

But Magnus shakes his head. "No," he says. "This is my fault. I've been so blind—just like the rest of them. Wanting to believe in the good of the organization. Going along with whatever they say, in an effort to protect my people. But now I see that under-neath the talk of modernization and reform, we're not much dif-ferent than the vampires of the past. Bloodthirsty, power-hungry, and ready to crush anyone who gets in our way."

He looks up at me, his eyes shining with unshed tears. "You have to believe me," he says. "I never knew they wanted to use your sister as bait. I never would have—"

"I know," I say, cutting him off. "I know you wouldn't do that to Rayne. Or to me. Or to Jareth."

"And that's why I'll never be a good leader," Magnus says dejectedly. "Too much heart."

"No. That's why you *are* a good leader. Because you actually care about your people, not just power," I correct. I reach over and give him a loving squeeze. His body shudders in my arms.

A moment later, he pulls away. "I'll call Jareth," he says. "No matter what Pyrus threatens, we're not giving up Rayne without a fight."

I stare at him in horror. "But didn't you hear what Pyrus said? They'll stake you for treason if you interfere!"

He shrugs. "Then they'll stake me. I couldn't live with myself anyway, if I knew I didn't do everything in my power to save your sister."

"Oh, Magnus," I cry. "I love you so much. I'm sorry I ever doubted you."

"You had right to," he says. "But no longer."

22

"Aw, look, I think she likes me!" I coo as the tiny tabby crawls into my lap and looks up at me with big green cat eyes. I reach down to stroke her between her ears and she purrs contentedly.

"I think they all like you," Magnus grumps, glancing at his watch. The black cat near his feet hisses at the sudden movement. "And I think they all hate me."

I reach over and pull the black cat over to me. "It's okay, baby," I murmur. "Don't let that big bad vampire scare you." I look up at my boyfriend, who's brushing hair off his suit. "Sorry," I say. "But you gotta admit, Jareth's right. A cat café is pretty much the last place we'd accidentally run into any Consortium members."

Calico, the cat café in Shinjuku we're currently holed up in, is pretty much exactly what it sounds like: a small café, filled with cats and kittens. For Japanese men and women who work long hours and can't have their own pet, it's like a furry oasis in the center of downtown. They get their animal fix and they don't have to deal with kitty litter.

And, since vampires, as I mentioned, aren't so good with animals, it's a great place to hide away and plot out our plan to save my sister.

The door opens and Jareth steps inside, his face haggard and his hair wild. He brushes the cat hair off the bench and sits down next to Magnus.

"Okay, here's what I've been able to find out," he says, getting right down to business. "They know where the Alphas are holed up, but the address is available to highest security clearance only. All I could figure out was it's some kind of temple."

"That doesn't help us much," Magnus replies. "There are hundreds of temples in the city."

"Well, they're making plans to bomb this one," Jareth informs us. "Just before dawn. Which doesn't give us much time to figure it out."

"Bomb it?" I repeat in horror. "But they can't! Not with Rayne inside!"

Jareth rakes a hand through his hair. "What does Pyrus care?" he asks bitterly. "He was ready to sacrifice her from the beginning. After she did everything they asked. Went to rehab, fixed her blood problem—and for what? So they'd have a better bargaining chip?" He narrows his eyes, gripping the side of his chair so tightly that the plastic crumbles in his hand and a calico cat hisses menacingly at him. "I can't even explain what it was like," he continues. "Going in there, pretending I was on that egomaniac's side so he'd give the Blood Coven to me and not one of their other flunkies who might not have its best interest at heart.

Just looking at his self-satisfied smirk as I swore allegiance, I wanted to stake him right then and there. Thank goodness he has no idea of my personal relationship with Rayne."

Magnus reaches out and squeezes his shoulder sympathetically. "You did well," he says. "For the good of the coven. I'm sure it was difficult." He shakes his head. "We've been so blind, wanting this to work. But with Pyrus at the helm, the Consortium is acting no better than these Alphas are. All he cares about is being on top. Gaining power, ruling the world, even at the expense of his own members. And the other masters are so afraid of what will happen to their covens if they go against what he says . . ."

"By the way," Jareth says, "I found out something else interesting."

"Yes?"

"It was Pyrus who sent the order to England, under your name, to Tanner, asking that he poison Jayden. He felt as long as he was alive you'd continue to be distracted and seek out the Holy Grail, which was counterproductive to his war."

"Of course," Magnus says wearily. "I should have known. Tanner would never do something like that on his own. He's loyal to a fault."

"That bastard," I snarl, anger welling up inside of me. "What right does he have to decide who gets to live or die?" I turn to Magnus. "I'm sorry," I say. "I don't know how I could have ever thought you would be behind something like that. I'm the worst girlfriend in the world."

He smiles grimly. "You can make it up to me later. Right now we've got to figure out how to find and rescue Rayne before they bomb the Alphas out of oblivion."

"Well," I say, pulling two cats off my lap, "I do have an idea . . ."

The two vampires look at me eagerly and for a split second I feel a thrill of pride that they are actually now taking me seriously. Treating me like an equal instead of a child.

"Go on," Magnus urges.

"Well, we know that Corbin has been listening to Jayden's thoughts, which has kept him one step ahead of us this entire time."

"Right."

"Well, what if we plant some kind of thought in Jayden's head? Tell him some kind of secret location or something. And when Corbin goes there, we'll kidnap him and demand he bring us to their headquarters."

"That's not a bad idea," Jareth muses. "Though we'd need Jayden to believe what he's thinking. Otherwise Corbin may see through it. It's hard to hide one's true thoughts."

"I think you two are forgetting something," Magnus interjects. "They already have what they want from Jayden. Rayne's already their prisoner. Meaning Corbin's probably no longer listening in."

I frown, realizing he's right. "If only it worked the other way, too," I say with a sigh. "Then it'd be easy."

"What do you mean?"

"Well, we know that Corbin's stayed a step ahead of us because he can read Jayden's mind. It's just too bad Jayden can't read his mind back. Like two-way telepathy."

"Have you ever asked Jayden if he could?" Jareth asks suddenly.

I look up, surprised. "Well, no. I just figured . . ." I trail off.

Maybe he's right. Maybe Jayden can read Corbin's mind. "But don't you think he would have told me if he could?" I ask.

"Maybe he doesn't know he can," Jareth says. "Maybe it's not a conscious thing. But if there's some kind of link, we may be able to reverse it through hypnosis. If he's willing, I should be able to focus his mind and have him push the other direction. To see inside Corbin's head."

"You can do hypnosis?" I ask, eyes widening. "I had no idea."

He blushes. "When you've been around a thousand years, you tend to pick up a few random skills here and there."

"Nice. Have you ever considered hypnotizing my sister?"

"Why? You want her to cluck like a chicken?"

"I'm thinking bigger picture. Like give her the undeniable urge to pick up after herself. Especially in our shared bedroom."

Magnus rolls his eyes. "Focus, people," he interjects. "Sunny, do you think Jayden would be amenable to this?" he asks. "It won't be easy if he's not a willing subject."

My mind flashes back to Jayden. His declarations of devotion. Our secret kiss. The look on his face when I walked out of the ryokan, leaving him behind. "Yes," I reply. "He feels terrible about what he's done and will do whatever it takes, I'm sure, to set things right. I mean, it wasn't like he did all of this on purpose. He just wanted to—" I stop short, realizing I haven't actually revealed this part of the story to my boyfriend.

Magnus looks at me pointedly. "He wanted to . . . ?" he prods.

"He just wanted to get me to like him," I admit. "He thought he'd have a better chance with me if he were a vampire."

Magnus rolls his eyes. "Stupid kid," he says scornfully. "I mean, everyone who knows you knows you pretty much can't stand vampires."

"I don't know," I say with a small smile. "They're growing on me."

Jareth rises to his feet. "Okay," he says. "Let's head to your hotel and find Jayden. We're running out of time and we must save your sister."

23

"Jayden, are you here?" I ask, bursting into our ryokan bed-room, Jareth and Magnus hot on my heels. In my haste I don't even bother to take off my shoes—a definite faux pas—and end up regrettably trouncing a great deal of mud into the room.

I scan the small area, my eyes falling on Jayden standing by the window, staring out into the night. Thank goodness he's still here. He turns as he hears me, his expression more than a bit nervous. Especially when Magnus and Jareth step into the room after po-litely taking off their own shoes. They have such better manners than me.

"Sunny!" he cries. "You . . . you came back."

"Of course I did," I assure him as guilt starts clawing at my gut. What, did he think I was going to leave him here forever? Never speak to him again? I guess in a way he deserves it. But I know what he did was out of love. And we've all done stupid things out of love. "I couldn't just leave you here, now, could I?"

His shoulders slump. "Well, to be honest, I wouldn't have blamed you if you did. I mean, I pretty much screwed everything up. All those people at Bite Club were killed—because of me. All those vampires staked. And your sister . . ." He hangs his head. "I've been staring out the window, waiting for dawn. So I can walk outside and burn myself to death. After what I've done, I don't deserve to live."

"Oh, Jayden, don't say things like that," I plead, horror washing over in a wave. "We've all made mistakes. And we may be able to set this right—and save my sister. But we need your help."

His eyes brighten. "Yeah? I'll do anything. *Anything.* I know I can't make up for all I've done, but whatever I can do to help . . . I'll do it." He looks at me with an agonized expression on his beautiful face, which breaks my heart. I want to be furious with him. But how can I?

"Sunny, why isn't he tied up?" Magnus demands in a tight voice, giving Jayden a suspicious once-over. "I told you, new vampires can be—"

"Dangerous, unpredictable, I know, I know," I finish for him. "But Jayden's learned self-control. He's fine. He doesn't need to be treated like animal."

But even as I say the words, I see Jayden putting out his hands to the vampires in surrender. "Cuff me," he says to Magnus. "I don't want to hurt anyone anymore."

I turn to him, shocked. "But, Jayden!"

He gives me an apologetic smile. "Sunny, it's for my own good. And you know it."

And so I give in, allowing them to slide a pair of handcuffs on his wrists, rendering him immobile. I avert my eyes—the slight smoke rising from his flesh as the silver burns is too painful to watch.

"Let's just get this over with," I growl.

Jareth leads Jayden over to a futon mat and the two of them sit down across from each other. In a low voice, I hear him explaining how the hypnosis will work and what we'll be able to do with it.

"Are you ready?" Jareth asks Jayden. My friend nods. "Okay, close your eyes and count backward from ten."

"Ten . . . nine . . ." By the time Jayden reaches three, his eyes dull and facial muscles slack. He's under Jareth's control.

"Now, Jayden, I need you to search through your mind for me," Jareth instructs. "Look for something out of place. Some kind of dark hole you've never seen before. Maybe a cut in the fabric of reality. Some kind of wound. Do you see anything like that?"

Jayden moans. "Sunny . . ."

"I'm right here," I cry, dropping to my knees. "Are you okay?"

"Sunny, don't hate me."

I swallow hard. "I don't hate you, Jayden. I could never hate you."

Silence, then, "But you're sorry you kissed me."

Damn. I can feel Magnus's eyes burning a hole in my backside. Maybe I can tell him Jayden meant that old kiss back in Vegas. That he's still holding on to some residual guilt from that.

But no. If I expect Magnus to tell me the truth, I need to give him the same respect. I will tell him what happened. I have to give him that much.

But not now. We can't afford to be distracted by petty jealousy. So instead, I turn to Jareth. "Can we get him to focus here?" I ask. "We don't have much time."

Jareth makes a face but nods, taking Jayden's hands into his own. "Jayden," he whispers. "I need you to focus on that hole. The one Corbin climbs through at night to read your thoughts. Do you see it?"

Jayden squeezes his eyes shut, then blinks a few times. Finally, he nods excitedly. "There's a small burn," he announces. "Near the back of my brain. It looks new. And . . . well, infected, I guess. Kind of juicy."

My stomach roils. TMI big-time, Jayden. But Jareth gives us a thumbs-up. "Now, Jayden," he continues, "I want you to crawl down that hole. Down the dark tunnel until you see the light on the other side. Can you do that for me?"

Jayden nods, blinking furiously now. "It's so dark," he moans. "So black. So full of hate."

"Yup, that sounds like Corbin's brain, all right," I can't help but interject. The two vampires shoot me warning looks.

"Look through his eyes, Jayden. What do you see?"

"A . . . temple," Jayden replies, after giving it some thought. "I think it's some kind of ancient temple."

"Good boy," Jareth encourages, even though we knew that part already. "But I need more details. Things about the temple Corbin knows. Search his brain. What do you see?"

"It's large, painted red and gold. There are paper lanterns hanging from the ceiling," he explains slowly. "There are many people wandering about. Tourists. Worshipers. They write down prayers and burn them in the fire in hopes they will be answered. They think the temple is a place of good. They don't know its inner secrets. Corbin longs for their innocence."

"Yeah, I bet he does," I mutter.

Jareth squeezes Jayden's hands. "A name, Jayden, I need a name. Or a neighborhood, at least. Where is this temple Corbin is looking at? What's its name?"

My friend moans loudly, shaking his head from side to side. "It's there," he says, "but it's hidden. He doesn't want me to see. He doesn't want anyone to see his plan." He cries out in horror. "What is he going to do? No! I can't look anymore. His mind is too black!"

"Jayden, come on!" I plead. "Please! My sister's life is at stake here!"

"He can't hear you, Sunny," Magnus whispers.

Jayden rocks back and forth, his forehead etched with distress, his eyes squeezed shut. "The temple . . ." he tries. "The temple . . . the temple is called . . ."

We all three lean forward in anticipation.

"Sensō-ji," he murmurs in scarcely a whisper.

Then he falls back onto the mat in a deep faint.

24

Fortunately for us, the Sensō-ji temple is right in the ryokan's neighborhood of Asakusa and we're able to get there in about ten minutes on foot, dashing through neon-lit streets, past karaoke bars and loud, clanging pachinko parlors until we reach the compound. We enter through a massive red "thunder gate" flanked by statues and adorned with a gigantic red paper lantern, as Jayden had described, and enter a different era of Japan. The neon lights fade away, replaced by a narrow gauntlet of tiny shops that probably haven't changed much since ancient pilgrims used to traverse them, on their way to pray to Buddha for their hearts' desires. (Though their wares, back in the old days, may not have included so many Hello Kittys or cell phone cases.) Of course, at three in the morning, everything's closed and even the most dedicated of tourists have long since gone to bed.

At last we reach an equally impressive two-story inner gate, which, according to the signs, is known as the Hozo-mon. More lanterns hang from its rafters as well as an inexplicable pair of giant-sized sandals. To the right is a five-story pagoda, rising high into the sky.

I give a low whistle. "This place is incredible," I murmur to Jareth and Magnus. "I can't believe the Alphas picked this as their HQ."

"It's because it's holy ground," Magnus explains and I suddenly realize he's sweating profusely. "Contrary to popular belief, it's not just the Christian religion—crosses and Holy Water—that affect us. In fact, any religious icons or land deemed sacred by mortals can weaken a vampire."

I look at him, concerned. "Is that going to be a problem?"

"It is if you were counting on us using vampire powers to rescue your sister," Jareth interjects, also looking as if he's suddenly come down with the flu. "We're about at mortal strength now. The farther we go into the temple, the weaker we'll be."

"Well, I guess it's good you brought along a fairy," I reply smugly. But inside, I'm worried. How are we ever going to get Rayne out if my two superheroes are as weak as little lambs?

We had to leave Jayden behind at the ryokan, of course, seeing what a liability he'd be if Corbin decided to go and rescan his brain. But we untied him first and Jareth even hooked him up with some fake memories through hypnosis, once he woke up from his faint. If Corbin does decide to go spying, he's going to be pretty bored watching Jayden playing pachinko down at the local arcade.

"How do we get in?" Jareth wonders aloud, studying the second gate with a critical eye. "This place is huge."

I nod, taking it all in. The Alphas could be holed up in any one of the structures. Or all of them, for that matter. How do we find out where they're keeping my sister?

Suddenly, as if in answer, I catch a flash of red out of the corner of my eye. I whirl around. "Look!" I cry, pointing to a red-cloaked individual sprinting across the yard. "Either Little Red Riding Hood's come to Japan on vacation or that's an Alpha we can follow."

The vampires nod and we creep down the street, keeping the red cloak in our sights. The figure ducks behind a prayer tree and around the gate until he stops in front of a large blank wall. He knocks twice and to my surprise, the wall creaks open, revealing a passageway into the darkness. Score! The man steps inside and the wall slides closed again.

"I knew there had to be some kind of secret entrance," I exclaim excitedly. "Come on, let's go!"

"You can't just waltz in there," Magnus reminds me. "Especially if you're a vampire."

"He's right," Jareth agrees. "We'll stick out like a sore fang if we walk in there like this. And without our vampire powers, we're screwed."

I open my mouth to speak, but snap it shut as I hear someone else approaching. The three of us dive behind a nearby fence and watch as two more red-cloaked individuals stroll toward the doorway. Jareth looks at Magnus and nods, and before I even realize what's going on, they step out and face the two men. They may not have vampire strength, but they do have the element of surprise and a thousand years of practice. Knocking the two men out cold before they can scream, they drag them back behind the fence and strip them of their cloaks.

"Nice trick," I say, stepping out of my hiding place. "But I can do one better." I close my eyes and try to visualize the face of one of the Alphas. A moment later, I smile at Jareth and Magnus, a full-on Leanna imitator if there ever was one, right down to her

Victorian skirt and leather corset. "Now, boys," I say with a grin, "step right this way." I walk boldly up to the secret door and knock as I saw the first guy do.

A moment later a pair of eyes peeks out of the peephole. I smile widely. "It's me, Leanna," I say in an impatient voice. "Hurry up."

The gate slides open and the guard ushers us inside. He bows low to me, then turns to the two vampires with a suspicious gaze. "Who are you?" he demands. "Do you have ID?"

"What?" I cry, butting in and stepping between him and the two vampires. "Are you new or something? You don't recognize an Alpha when you see one?"

The guard blushes. "Sorry, Miss Leanna," he apologizes. "I mean no disrespect."

"I should hope not," I scold. "Or next time I shall be forced to speak to Roberta about your . . . memory problems." I cross my fingers that the old headmistress from back at Riverdale is still leading this motley crew.

Evidently so, from the way the guard stammers and shakes. "Please don't," he begs. "She'll take away my Alpha status. And I won't get to take the sacrament tonight with everyone else."

The sacrament? Does that have something to do with the theft of the Holy Grail? "Don't worry," I assure him in my most benevolent voice. "I'll say nothing. If, of course, you do me a favor and let me know where Corbin is. I have a message for him."

The guard's face betrays his ultimate relief. If he weren't a bad guy, I'd feel sorry for him right about now. "Of course," he agrees eagerly, swiping the sweat from his brow. "He's down in the basement lab with Dr. Franken. They're preparing the sacrament."

The sacrament again. What are the Alphas planning?

"Thank you," I say. "I'll go see him at once."

I beckon the boys to follow me and we all step into the elevator and I hit the only floor marked. The elevator begins its descent.

"Okay, we'll split up once we get down below," Jareth instructs. "Hunt for this so-called sacrament room. If you find Rayne, text us your location and we'll get her out of there."

I nod as the elevator doors slide open into a long dark, narrow corridor. But just as we're about to step out, none other than Corbin himself, flanked by four other red-hooded initiates I don't recognize, turns the corner. My fingers fumble with the "close door" button, but it's no use. His eyes alight upon me and he holds out a hand, blocking the doors.

"There you are!" he cries. "I've been looking everywhere for you. Come, we're almost ready to begin."

He grabs me by the arm and tries to lead me away. Behind me I can hear Magnus and Jareth try to follow. But Corbin stops and turns to them. "I just need Leanna," he says. "The rest of you need to head to the ceremony. We'll be ready to begin soon."

The four other initiates nod and gesture for Jareth and Magnus to follow them. They have no choice—without their vampire strength, they'd be no match for four trained slayers—and reluctantly start walking down the hall in the other direction, glancing behind them as they go.

"Where are they going?" I ask Corbin as he hustles me down the hall.

"To the temple, of course," he says, looking surprised. "Everyone's gathered for the sacrament. I figured that's where you were leading them."

"Oh, right, yeah. That's what I was doing."

We make a few turns down a narrow, closed-in hallway with low ceilings, which gives me major claustrophobia all over again. And this time I don't have Jayden there to hold my hand. I try to keep my breathing normal, though my heart's beating a thousand miles a minute. Where is Corbin taking me? Does he really buy my disguise or am I walking into a trap?

Finally, we stop in front of an old wooden door, covered in kanji symbols. Corbin pushes it open and ushers me inside. It appears to be some kind of prayer room that's been turned into a makeshift laboratory, with test tubes bubbling over Bunsen burners and vials of red liquid stashed on almost every available surface. Evidently the Night School experiments are continuing here in Japan.

But I disregard all the mess. Because in the center of the room is the pièce de résistance. The Holy Grail itself, sitting inside a formative-looking glass case. And behind it, strapped to a hospital bed, is my sister.

My breath catches in my throat as my eyes search her body for signs of life. I let out a sigh of relief as I catch a slight rise and fall of her chest. She looks weak and unconscious. But she's alive. We're not too late.

Though, at the moment, I'm in no position to do any rescuing . . .

"Look how cute she is when she's asleep," Corbin sneers, walking over to Rayne and poking her nastily. I dig my fingernails into my palm, forcing myself to stay in character. I can't fight Corbin by myself. I need to figure out another way.

"So how does the whole sacrament thing work again?" I ask, stalling for time, hoping it's not a dumb question.

"Why, it's quite simple, my dear," says a new voice. Behind Corbin, I see another man walk into the lab. A total mad-scientist type in desperate need of a good eyebrow wax. I remember Rayne talking about a Dr. Franken back at Night School. This must be the guy.

"It is?"

"Absolutely," he says, evidently proud of his plan. The bad guys always are, aren't they? "Each initiate will get a few drops of vamshee blood, followed by a chaser of Holy Grail."

Oh-kay then. "And . . . why the Holy Grail again? I mean, won't that just destroy the vampire cells?"

"It will suppress them, yes. But not destroy them," replies Dr. Franken. "Which is exactly what we need when injecting a vampire/fairy blood cocktail into our subjects. Otherwise the vampire blood cells will start attacking the human cells too quickly—destroying them before they have a chance to bond with the fairy ones and grow strong enough to survive." He shakes his head sorrowfully. "Leaving our poor candidates in very bad shape. Most likely comatose."

I shudder, remembering all the bodies back in Night School—the failed experiments. "But the Holy Grail will fix all that?" I ask, wishing I'd paid better attention in chemistry class.

Corbin nods. "Yes. That, combined with the weakening effects of being on sacred ground, will give the fairy cells a chance to bond with the human ones. Then, as the Grail suppressant wears off, the vampire cells will regain their strength. But, by that time, the fairy/human cell compound has already grown strong and all the cells will have no choice but to work together."

"And then," Dr. Franken finishes triumphantly, "we will have successfully created an all-powerful vamshee, a creature with the powers of both the vampire and the fairy. The most exquisite—and deadly—creature the Earth has ever seen."

"We've already had three successful transformations tonight," Corbin adds. "And now it's time to start building our army."

Dr. Franken cackles. "Those stupid Consortium vampires won't know what hit them," he says. "They'll be surrendering quicker than you can say 'fresh blood.'" He rubs his hands together in glee. "Now, if you'll excuse me, I have some last-minute preparations to make." He bows his head, then turns to leave the room.

Once he's gone, Corbin grabs my hands in his own cold ones and dances around the room, pulling me with him. "That was great!" he tells me. "You played your part perfectly! Dr. Franken thinks we're completely on board with his stupid plan!" He laughs loudly. "If only he knew!"

Huh? I'm so confused now. Corbin's double-crossing the Alphas? Could he be a good guy all along? Maybe even working for the Consortium as a double agent?

Before I can open my mouth to ask the questions, Corbin leans down and plants a kiss on my lips. "Aren't you excited, my love?" he breathes.

"Excited about what?" asks a voice through the doorway.

I look up just in time to see the real Leanna step into the lab. Oh, crap.

25

So I might not have mentioned this before, but there's one major downside to fairy shape-shifting. Namely, if you run into the person you're currently shape-shifted as, well, the illusion shatters instantly, leaving you looking just like your old miserable self again. Which is exactly what happens to me, the second the real Leanna steps into the room.

"You!" Corbin cries, a look of horror washing over his face as he suddenly realizes he just basically gave away his entire evil plan to his number-one enemy.

"What's going on here?" Leanna demands. "Why is the vamshee not tied up?"

"It's not her, it's her meddling little sister," Corbin growls. "Get her!"

I glance desperately around the room, begging for an escape route, but unfortunately for me, Leanna's blocking the only way out and the ceilings are too low for me to take flight. Why, oh why, didn't I have the foresight to bring some sort of stake with me or something? Though I suppose that would only take out Corbin. I'd still have his little human girlfriend—not to mention a temple full of Alpha operatives—to contend with.

This is so not good.

Corbin grabs me from behind, pinning my arms to my sides. I try my best to squirm away, but even with his vampire strength subdued, he's still too strong. He drags me into the room's back closet and pushes me down onto an empty chair.

"Get me some rope," he instructs Leanna, who runs to comply. He looks down at me, his face twisted in hate. "Give me one good reason I shouldn't kill you now," he demands.

Fear pounds in my heart, my mind drawing a complete blank. I mean, sure, I can probably think of thousands of reasons I should stay alive, but likely none of them would work to sway him. ("I've never gotten to swim the English Channel," for example, just ain't going to cut it.)

Though there is something . . .

"Because I'm a fairy," I reply. "And girlfriend of the Blood Coven master. Which makes me a very valuable prisoner, in case something goes wrong with your oh-so-clever plan."

Corbin opens his mouth to reply—but Leanna returns at that moment with some rope and together the two of them set out to tie me up. I guess I should be thrilled right about now that he's evidently decided against killing me in cold blood, though, to be honest, I just can't seem to muster up the appropriate level of enthusiasm.

"What's your deal?" I demand, trying not to yelp as he yanks the cord tight around my wrist. "I thought you hated the Alphas after what they did to you. Why are you helping them now?"

Corbin nods to Leanna, who walks over and shuts the closet door. Then he turns to me. "Don't be ridiculous," he spits. "I'm not really helping them. And I'm certainly not going to let them create an army of disgusting monsters. Hell, the world's got enough vampires already. The last thing we need is an army of super-undead being run by crazy people who want to take over the world."

Slight hope rises within me. Maybe I was right—maybe he is actually a double agent. "Who are you working for then?" I demand.

"Please," he scoffs. "I work myself. And I'm going to get my revenge against every single person who did me wrong."

"And how are you going to do that?"

"Corbin, you're telling her too much," Leanna warns.

But Corbin just chuckles. "What can she do to stop me?" he says maliciously. So much for thinking he could be a good guy. He turns back to me. "Tonight, all the Alpha initiates are supposed to receive a drop of blood from your sister. The so-called sacrament. But what they don't know is that I've poisoned her blood."

My heart lurches. "What?"

"When they drink, they'll be poisoned, too," he continues, looking quite proud of himself. "This way I can wipe out the entire organization in one foul swoop. Then they'll be sorry they lied to me and my friends."

Wow. I don't know if that's good or bad . . .

"What about my sister?" I find myself saying. "She's not a part of this. Can you . . . um, poison them a different way or something?"

Corbin flashes his fangs at me and I recoil in horror. "Your sister?" he spits out. "Are you kidding me? If it wasn't for your sister and her bloody big appetite, I would have never been transformed into this horrible monster to begin with." He squeezes his hands into fists. "She deserves all that's coming to her and a lot more."

I let out a frustrated breath. "I know," I admit. "She did you wrong. But she paid for it, you know. She went to rehab and everything. She feels terrible about what she did."

"Well, she should," he huffs. "Though luckily I've figured out a way to reverse it all. Once I've finished here I'm heading back to Switzerland to meet up with my chemist friend. He can make the Holy Grail into a nice little antidote for me. I'll turn back into a human and live a happily-ever-after normal mortal life with Leanna here." He turns to the other Alpha and smiles at her fondly. Seriously, when did the two of them start hooking up?

Normal. I remember wanting that so badly . . . I almost feel bad for the guy. If, you know, he wasn't planning to kill me and my sister.

"Mortal or vampire, you'll never be normal," I spit out. "You'll always be a monster."

He lunges at me, but Leanna yanks him back just in time. "Come on," she says. "Don't waste your time with this nobody. We've got to get ready. The sacrament is scheduled to begin any moment now."

Corbin lets out a breath. "You're right," he says. Then he turns to me. "I'm going to enjoy disemboweling your sister," he spits. And then, with that lovely sentiment, he follows Leanna out, closing the door behind him and leaving me in darkness.

Once their footsteps fade away, I work to try to break my bonds. But it's no use. I'm stuck fast and I succeed only in making my wrists bleed. If only I had that kind of mental telepathy with Magnus that Rayne has with Jareth. Then at least I could warn him.

He and Jareth are probably out there right now in the cere-mony room with the other initiates, with no idea what's going on. Which means they might be forced to take a sip from my sister. And while I'm not sure if her poisonous blood can kill full-blooded vampires, I'm so not ready to take that chance. I've got to warn them somehow.

And then there's my sister. My sweet Rayne. My best friend in the world, lying unconscious on a table, her blood swimming with poison. If the poison doesn't kill her, the thousand bites from the initiates will drain her dry. And then she'll be gone . . . forever.

Meaning half of me will be gone, too.

A lump forms in my throat. I feel so damn helpless. If only there was a way to get out. I'd trade every bit of "normal" to just have some kind of crazy superpower right about now to get me out of this mess so I can save my family.

But just as I'm about to give in to my despair, the door squeaks open and light shines into the room. I look up, assuming it's Corbin or Leanna, back for more. But it's not.

It's Jayden.

26

"Oh my God! Jayden!" I cry. I don't think I could be happier to see anyone—even the Bergdorf shoe fairy—at this point. "How did you—?"

He runs into the room and goes right to work on my bindings. "When Jareth hypnotized me he opened a two-way link between me and Corbin," he explains as he unties. "Once you guys left I kept getting visions of him and what he was doing. Which was annoying, at first. Until I caught a glimpse of you and I realized you were in trouble." He yanks the rope free. "So, of course, I had to rescue you," he adds shyly. "I hope that's okay."

I leap from my seat, throwing my arms around him in a huge hug. "Thank you so much! I don't know what I would have done without you!"

He smiles his crooked smile. "You won't ever have to find out."

My heart melts at his naked vulnerability. Half of me just

wants to kiss him all over again. To tell him I forgive him. But it's more complicated than that. And I need to stay focused here.

"We have to go find Magnus and Jareth," I tell him. "Corbin's planning to poison everyone here."

Jayden nods and we rush out of the closet and back into the makeshift lab. The good news—it's now totally deserted. The bad news—my sister's gone, too. Which means they must have moved her body to the main hall for the ceremony. We don't have much time left.

But something out of the corner of my eye causes me to pause at the door. The Holy Grail. It's still sitting in its glass case. I run over, grabbing a metal bar off the counter, and start smashing at the glass.

"What are you doing?" Jayden cries.

The glass shatters. I reach in and pull out the cup. Then I try to hand it to him. "This is it," I tell him. "Drink this and you'll be mortal again. You won't have to live this vampiric nightmare anymore."

To my surprise Jayden refuses the goblet. "No," he says, shaking his head. "As long as I remain a vampire, I share Corbin's link. I can read his mind and help you defeat the Alphas and save your sister. I can't do that if I go back to being a weak-ass, powerless human."

"But . . ." My heart wrenches at his words. I know he's doing this for me. To prove his love. To offer protection at the expense of his own happiness. But the price he'll pay for his devotion may be too high to bear. "Look, Jayden, as much as I appreciate your willingness to help, you're running out of time. Once your vampire cells bond completely with your human ones, that's it. There's no turning back. What if this is your last chance to regain your mortality?"

He shrugs. "Then I'll miss my last chance. I'll deal."

He sounds so confident. And half of me wants to agree with him. Just let him be a vampire—my immortal protector—for the rest of eternity. But no, I can't do that to him. I can't let him make the ultimate sacrifice for me when I still don't even know what it is I want from him.

Once upon a time, I, too, had been tempted to give up my humanity for love. Not because I wanted to become a vampire. But because I wanted to be with Magnus. But Magnus realized this—and saved me from myself.

And now I have to do the same for Jayden. Or I'll never be able to live with myself.

"Can you listen to Corbin now?" I ask him. "Figure out which way he went?"

Jayden nods, closing his eyes to concentrate. I take the opportunity to swig a big gulp of the Grail. (Which, um, is completely nasty, by the way.)

Jayden opens his eyes, oblivious. "He's in some kind of big temple," he says. "Where they're holding the biting ceremony—"

I don't let him finish. Instead, I throw my arms around him and kiss him hard on the lips. His mouth opens in surprise, allowing me to let the liquid flow through.

He gags and jerks away, spitting it out. I hope he managed to swallow some . . .

"What the hell was that?" he demands.

"Jayden," I say softly, wiping the liquid from my own mouth. "I don't think you really want to be a vampire."

His eyes widen in realization. He stares at me. "You didn't . . ." he whispers. "Oh God, Sunny, you didn't!"

"I'm sorry," I say, my heart aching in my chest. "I know it was a low move. But I had no choice."

"Why would you do that?" he whispers. "I could have helped."

"You've helped enough," I assure him, tears falling from my eyes. "Now it's my turn to help you. Some of us are cursed with the darkness. But you still have a chance. A chance at a normal life, surrounded by the people and animals you love so much. They need you, Jayden. Your friends. The dogs and cats of the theater. And I think, deep down, if you're honest with yourself, you'll find you need them, too." I pause, then add, "And I refuse to be the selfish person who robs you of your life and everything you love."

"But I don't mind—"

"Maybe not now," I agree. "But someday you would. Someday you'd start to regret the sacrifice you made for me. And you'd start to resent me for that. Maybe even hate me a little. And I couldn't live with that."

Jayden says nothing at first, tears streaming down his cheeks, matching my own. Then, finally, he nods. "Oh, Sunny," he murmurs. "I'll never forget what you've done for me."

I reach out to pull him into a rough hug, my tears splashing down onto his shoulder. "That makes two of us."

27

After saying good-bye to Jayden and promising to call him the second this is all over, I conjure up another red robe, then sneak down the now-empty halls once again, this time following signs to the temple, where evidently everyone's gathering for the main event.

I step into the large chamber, a cavernous underground arena that would astound those who worship at the now-paltry-looking temple aboveground. The whole place seems as if it's been dipped in gold and draped with crimson curtains. Statues of Buddha are everywhere and smoke streams from incense being burned on several altars. I feel like I've snuck into the devil worshiper's place in *Indiana Jones and the Temple of Doom*. Except these initiates are wearing red cloaks and they're all facing a large, curtained stage at the front of the room in anticipation of the upcoming sacrament.

I scan the place, desperately seeking Magnus and Jareth—who texted to let me know they made it to the temple—but with everyone in matching outfits, it's harder to pick anyone out than in a *Where's Waldo?* book.

"Oh my God! Sunny McDonald? Is that you?" squeals a voice beside me.

Shocked at the sound of my name, I whirl around, my eyes widening as they fall on none other than my old friend Evelyn from back at Riverdale Academy, flanked by her Slay School friends Amber, Ember, Gwen, and Mackenzie. They're all wearing the requisite red robes and all excitedly clamor around me—hugging and squealing in excitement. While I greatly appreciate the sentiment and yes, I missed them, too, I'm wondering how I can politely let them know I need to keep a low profile here.

"I can't believe you got here!" Evelyn cries. "I thought somehow you got lost in the big move."

"Move?" I repeat, wondering what the Alpha group's cover story was to their students. After all, these girls signed up to be slayers to fight evil—not become it. There's no way they'd be down with the headmistress's plan for world domination if they knew what it entailed.

"Didn't you hear? That's why we're in Japan!" adds Amber, who appears to be wearing a Batman logo shirt under her robes. Jareth would be so pleased. "Remember that vampire who bit Corbin back at school? Well, she escaped and brought all her evil vampire friends back with her."

"It was awful!" cries Gwen. "We barely got out alive."

"Yeah, we had to take off in the middle of the night and leave all our stuff behind," Kenzie adds with a scowl.

I cringe. So that's what Headmistress Roberta told them? That the group moved them across the world for their own protection against vampires set to drain them dry? I guess that explains all the willing victims here.

"So what's all this about now?" I ask, wondering if they even know why they're here tonight. I mean, I can't imagine these innocent girls would willingly give their lives to the cause and become vampiric fae.

The girls look at one another, then back at me. Ember lowers her voice. "We don't know," she hisses. "All we know is there's supposed to be something they're calling 'the sacrament' that we all have to take."

"And once we do," Amber adds, "we can finally graduate to fully licensed slayers."

"I cannot wait to graduate," Gwen says passionately. "Then maybe I can finally go home."

"Since the vampire attack, we've been on total lockdown," adds her cousin Kenzie. "We're not allowed to contact any friends or family not affiliated with the organization." She frowns. "I never thought I'd miss my mom so much."

I bite my lower lip, wondering what on Earth I should tell them. If I can't stop Corbin from doling out the poisoned blood, these innocent girls will die. And if I do stop him, they're still in danger of being bombed to oblivion by the Consortium in just a few hours.

"Um, what if you guys left now?" I try, without much hope. "I mean, you all miss your families, right? Why don't you just skip out on this whole crazy sacrament thing and go home to see them?"

"Leave?" Evelyn looks at me like I'm crazy. "But we've worked so hard to get here! And we're finally going to graduate. How could we just leave?"

"Besides, we've all taken a vow to kill evil vampires," Amber reminds me. "After all, if we slayers don't stand together against the darkness of the otherworld, who will?"

Good question. And right about now, it's looking like yours truly is the prime candidate. After all, as much as I hate what the Alphas are doing to my sister, I can't in good conscience let all these innocent people die. They may be slayers, but they're good kids who have somehow found themselves unknowingly on the wrong side. I'm sure if we were able to get them away they'd make valuable members of the real Slayer Inc. organization. The one run by Vice President Teifert, who is only interested in upholding justice and the law, not trying to take over the world.

But, I realize at the same time, even if we could pry them away from the Alpha's clutches, the Consortium would still not likely let them live. It would be a risk. And I've seen firsthand what the Consortium thinks of taking risks. To them, the only good slayer is a dead slayer.

Of course, at the moment, it's not up to them, now, is it?

"I've got to go do something," I tell my friends. "But I need you guys to do me a major favor."

"What's that?" Gwen asks.

"Promise me when the ceremony starts, you'll go stand near the exit. Then if something . . . were to go wrong . . . you can get out easily."

They stare at me with wide, confused eyes. "Go wrong?" Ember asks. "What could go wrong?"

"I can't explain now," I apologize. "But trust me, okay?"

They all nod and turn to slowly push their way through the crowd, toward the back doors. I let out a sigh of relief. Well, that's something, at least.

But now I have bigger fish to fry. I weave through the crowd, toward the front of the stage. Suddenly a rough hand grabs me and yanks me to the sidelines. What now? I whirl around, my eyes thankfully alighting on Magnus.

"You scared me!" I hiss.

He grabs me roughly and pulls me close, squeezing me so tight for a moment I think he's going to crush my ribs. Guess that means I'm forgiven for my Jayden-kissing sins.

"I was worried!" he cries, kissing the top of my head over and over. "We kept trying to text you and you didn't answer. And the guards wouldn't let us leave the chamber once we walked in. I thought . . ." His voice cracks. "Well, I thought you were . . ."

I reach out to squeeze his hand. "Well, once again you underestimated your little Sunshine," I tease. "I'm totally fine. But we have bigger problems." In a low voice, I give him and Jareth the rundown of what I learned from Corbin. Jareth cringes when I mention Rayne's poisoning.

"Okay," Jareth says when I'm finished. "So we'll find where they've got her stashed, grab her, and get the hell out of here so the Consortium can blast the lot of them to kingdom come. Sound good?"

I bite my lower lip. "Um, no," I say. "I'm not okay with that, actually."

The vampires stare at me in disbelief. "What?" Magnus asks. "Sunny, why not?"

"Look, there are a lot of innocent people here, okay?" I remind them. "Sure, the leaders are evil and all that. But the rest of them are just students. Pawns in the Alphas' game. They never signed up to become vamshee warriors. They don't want to take over the world. They just want to help police the bad guys—like my sister and my stepmom and my mom's boyfriend, David, and all the others in the main Slayer Inc. group. They don't deserve to be poisoned. And they certainly don't deserve to be bombed by the Consortium either."

"I suppose you would have tried to save the construction workers on the Death Star, as well," Jareth replies drolly.

"Hey! All those guys wanted to do was feed their families . . ."

Magnus scowls. "If we let them go free, the war will continue indefinitely. And the Alphas will gain the upper hand."

"I don't believe that," I say stubbornly. "I think if we tell these people what's really going on, they'll rebel against the leaders who lied to them. They'll turn to our side."

"It's a dangerous gamble you're asking for," Jareth growls. "Do you really believe all these people here are innocent?"

"I lived with them at Riverdale, remember?" I ask. "They're good kids. They've just been lied to and tricked. And once they find out what's really going on, I don't believe a single one of them will side with Headmistress Roberta."

"That's all well and good, but—"

I turn to Magnus. "Look, you're always asking me to see the bigger picture," I remind him. "And yes, I want to save my sister. More than anything in the world. But I can't do it at the expense of having hundreds of other innocent people killed instead."

Magnus sighs. "Did I ever mention you're too good for your own good?"

I grin. "All the time."

"Well, whatever we do, we need to make a decision fast," Jareth says, glancing at his watch. "Because the bombs will start flying in less than an hour."

I open my mouth to reply, but at that moment I'm cut off

as the trumpets sound and the red silk curtain slowly slides open. The crowd erupts in excited cheers and whoops as none other than Headmistress Roberta herself steps up to the podium, illuminated by a single spotlight.

It's showtime.

28

I watch as the headmistress's lips curl into a self-satisfied smirk as the crowd continues to cheer her on. She's wearing a dramatically low-cut red silk gown and boasts glittery jewelry at her fingers, ears, and throat. Gone are the bun and thick glasses; she's now very Dame Helen Mirren at the Golden Globes and a far cry from her normal Riverdale schoolmarm chic. I guess if you're a super-villain with a plot to take over the world, at some point you have to start dressing the part.

She raises her hands to the crowd and the cheering intensifies. Poor sheep. If only they knew what their mistress is really asking them to sign up for. But, of course, they don't, and so they keep applauding, as if she's going to give away free tickets to a Lady Gaga show to the loudest fan.

With a swish of her wrist, she cuts them off—and silence blankets the room. She clears her throat before speaking. The anticipation is so thick you could cut it with a stake.

"My dear slayers," she says, purring into the microphone. "It's so good to see all of you gathered here today, united as one front against the evil forces that threaten to batter down our doors. For far too long has Slayer Inc. been a puppet organization, content to do the dirty work for supernatural beings who harbor no appreciation for all that's done for them. But those days are now over." She pauses, for effect, and her audience mindlessly cheers.

"Are you sure they're worth saving?" Magnus mutters at my side. I shush him.

The headmistress continues, "Once upon a time we were able to peacefully coexist with the various vampire covens around the world," she says. "Enforcing their laws, protecting humanity from harm. But now the Consortium of vampires has grown in number—not to mention hunger for power. They are no longer interested in living under the rules of a nonpartisan police force. Mainly because they are no longer interested in playing by the rules to begin with. Rules, I think we can all agree, were created for the sole purpose of keeping the peace and bettering our society."

"You know, she's not entirely wrong," I hear Magnus grudgingly whisper to Jareth. "There was a time when all Consortium members had a real vote. A chance to voice our opinion without fear of repercussions. Now, if you happen to have a differing opinion to Pyrus, you're bound to be ostracized and punished as I have been."

"I suppose you're right," Jareth relents. "But what can we possibly do about it? I mean, the Blood Coven is not strong enough to go out on its own without the protection of a larger entity."

"I think the Blood Coven is stronger than you might think."

"Guys! Can we please discuss politics later?" I hiss. "I need to hear this speech."

I tune back in to the headmistress. "I know recently we had a major setback," she admits. "The Night School program was infiltrated by a vampire, out to destroy all the work we've been doing to protect our society. As those of you from Riverdale know, we barely escaped with our lives. But now we've regrouped and, thanks to a few exceptional Alphas in our midst, we're stronger than ever and ready to take this campaign to the next level." She pauses, smiling widely as the crowd once again erupts into the requisite applause.

"And now I'd like to introduce you to one of them," she continues. "He started at Riverdale like any other Slayer in Training, but rose quickly through the ranks, becoming the best pupil we had by far—both on the field and in the classroom.

"Of course his excellence made him a prime target for the vampire spy. She seduced him, captured him, even tried to kill him. But, students, the skills he learned at Riverdale Academy allowed him to escape and bring back valuable information we will use against the Consortium." She turns offstage. "Ladies and gentlemen, I give you Corbin Billingsworth the Third!"

Now the crowd is really freaking out as Corbin steps onto the stage, flashing the audience a cocky grin and swishing his crimson cape with an overly dramatic flair. He strolls over to Headmistress Roberta and hugs her tightly, as if she's his mentor and best friend in the world. Ha! If only she knew! Her little protégé is more conniving than ten vampires put together. Not to mention a total traitor to her illustrious cause.

Corbin releases her and turns to face the crowd. The arrogance on his face is completely over-the-top. But the audience doesn't seem to mind. They've fallen hook, line, and sinker for this guy, looking up to him with enraptured faces, as if he's some kind of god, or at least Justin Bieber. I resist the nearly overwhelming urge to roll my eyes.

"Hello, Tokyo!" he cries into the mic, as if he's a rock-n-roller giving a concert. "Or should I say *konichiwa*?"

I suppose I don't have to tell you, but the crowd, predictably, goes wild. I'm betting half of these kids have Corbin pinup posters in their lockers.

"Thank you all for coming today," he says after the crowd finally calms down. "As Roberta said, we are currently at war, under siege by an undead army. And we must stick together to bear this storm. The vampires are coming and my spies say they're coming soon. We must be ready for them. And so I am asking you here, tonight, to make a pledge of commitment to our cause, by drinking the holy sacrament we are offering to you this day."

The crowd erupts in murmurs, probably trying to figure out, once again, what the heck this so-called sacrament could be.

Corbin motions to his two assistants, who, in response, hurry to the back of the stage. They grab hold of the ends of a giant red silk sheet, then yank it down in unison. The crowd gasps as the sheet falls away, revealing my sister, bound to a giant stone altar.

"Rayne!" Jareth cries hoarsely. I have to grab his arm to keep him from running forward in an insane attempt to rescue his blood mate.

"Hang on," I hiss. "We have to be smart about this."

Jareth reluctantly hangs back. But I can tell it's nearly impossible for him to fight the urge to save my sister. Which is admirable, if not stupid. I need to figure out my next move, pronto.

"This girl—this vampire," Corbin spits, "is the one who betrayed us all. The vamshee who snuck into our school and seduced us all into thinking she was just some normal slayer. But in reality, this monster was nothing more than a killer. A terrorist sleeper cell, biding her time, waiting to make her move and destroy us all when we least expected it."

To my dismay, the crowd totally seems to be buying it. They boo and hiss at my sister and a few shoes are even lobbed on-stage. One, in particular, connects with Rayne's stomach and she moans in pain, causing even more jeering from the crazy peanut gallery. I can't help but be reminded of *The Lion, The Witch, and the Wardrobe* book when the White Witch and her followers sacrifice Aslan. Problem is, unlike the lion in the story, I'm pretty sure my sister can't resurrect herself if she's killed.

"You are right to hate the evil one," Corbin says to the crowd, giving Headmistress Roberta a small smile. "But now that we have her under our control, she is going to help us rather than hurt us. Every one of us is going to partake of a single drop of her blood, chased by a purifying drop of the Holy Grail. And once those two bloods—one tainted, one pure—are inside your veins, you will gain the power to stand with us for the final battle against the vampires!"

He raises his hands again, as if expecting more cheers. But he misjudged his audience this time. Instead of excitement, I see worried glances and whispered fear. Seems like while everyone in the crowd is down for a good witch hunt, they draw the line at imbibing her bodily fluids, go figure.

"Um, but won't we turn into vampires if we drink it?" dares one guy at the back of the room.

Headmistress Roberta nods at Corbin, then takes the micro-phone from him. "Please." She sniffs. "You will become far more powerful than a mere vampire. You will become the ultimate slayer. An essential part of our war against all that is wrong in the world."

More discontented murmurs from the peanut gallery.

"Does this mean we can't go out in sunlight?" demands a girl to the right. "'Cause, like, how am I going to go visit my family in Jamaica if I can't go out in sunlight?"

"And do we have to drink blood?" adds Evelyn, who thankfully I realize is right up by the back door as she promised. "'Cause I faint at the sight of blood."

I can see Corbin grit his teeth. This is not how he expected things to go. "Fools," he hisses. "Don't you see what an honor it is to be chosen? You worry about silly, petty things. But look at the big picture. You will become responsible for saving thousands of lives. Protecting your family and friends from a life of mortal slavery at the hands of those who see them as nothing more than cattle, ready to be bled for their own foul purposes. You will be as you trained so long to be—on the front lines of a supernatural war." He shakes his head, as if disgusted by the lot of them. "I thought you were soldiers," he spits. "Real soldiers make sacrifices for their country—for their world. Don't you want the opportunity to make your world a better, safer place?"

Judging from the faces in the audience, I'm thinking there are quite a few people who wouldn't mind missing out on that particular honor and privilege. And they don't know the half of it. I can't believe Corbin has the gall to stand up there and lie to them all in his crazy quest for revenge. Even Headmistress Roberta, at least, thinks she's on a mighty crusade. He's just a vengeful dick who can't get over his Mommy and Daddy issues.

Time to make my move.

"I'll be back," I whisper to Jareth and Magnus, pushing my way toward the stage, trying to keep a low profile.

"All right, so if you can all form a line, we will begin the sacrament," Headmistress Roberta instructs. Evidently the time for debate is through. The Slayers in Training shuffle to obey, not looking all too pleased. But what choice do they have? The doors are locked. The guards have swords. They're in a foreign country and they have no place else to go.

Corbin smirks, then walks over to my sister, still prostrate on the altar, and pulls out a large silver knife. He slashes her leg and places a jeweled cup underneath. Blood gushes from the wound and into the cup. It's all I can do to keep from throwing up.

"Wait!" I cry, leaping onto the stage, just as the first victim steps toward Corbin and his cup.

The audience gasps, probably thinking they're seeing double. The guards lunge at me, but I leap into the air, using my wings to gain altitude. Once I'm above grabbing distance, I turn to the crowd, beating my wings to stay afloat. "Don't drink!" I cry. "She's been poisoned. You won't turn into vamshees. You'll just die!"

Corbin's face twists in rage. "She's lying!" he cries. "She's one of them. Look at her wings." He turns to the guards. "What are you standing around for? Get her!"

I turn to Headmistress Roberta, who's staring at me with confusion clear on her face. "Look," I say. "I don't agree with your methods, believe me. But there's more going on here than you know. Corbin's betrayed you. He's poisoned my sister's blood, and anyone who takes a sip will die before ever becoming some supernatural vamshee-warrior type."

Corbin shoots me a death look. "That's ridiculous," he entreats the headmistress. "Why would I want to poison my own people?"

"Because you feel they betrayed you first," I reply smugly. "They experimented on your friends. Turned them into vegetables before they perfected their formula. And they would have done the same thing to you, if you hadn't escaped with Rayne."

"Rayne," Corbin spits out. "Rayne nearly killed me. Because of her I'm a blasted creature of the night."

"Exactly," I say. "And there's nothing you hate more than vampires. After all, your parents were killed by one. There's no way you'd just let the Alphas create hundreds more vampire hybrids when your life's mission is to wipe all supernatural beings off the face of the Earth."

Headmistress Roberta gives Corbin a hard stare. "Is this true?" she demands.

"No! Of course not!"

"Prove it."

Corbin rolls his eyes. "Fine. I'll drink it myself." He puts the cup to his lips.

"No." Roberta yanks it from his grasp. "You think I was born yesterday?" she sniffs. "Being a vampire grants you immunity from the poison." She scans the group of frightened initiates, her eyes alighting on Leanna. "Come up here, child," she urges.

Leanna looks at her, face white as a ghost. "What?" she cries. "I mean . . . no!"

"Oh, yes," Roberta says with a small smile. "Guards?" The guards grab her by both arms and drag her, kicking and screaming, to the front of the stage. Roberta strolls over and puts the cup to Leanna's trembling lips. Then she turns to Corbin.

"Tell me the truth, now," she says with tight lips. "Or your little girlfriend here will have to prove your innocence the hard way."

Corbin glowers at her for a moment. Then his face twists into an angry mask of hate. "Fine," he spits out. "She's right. I did poison the bitch. No vampire deserves to live."

The crowd gasps in horror. Roberta simply nods, then tips the cup back, forcing Leanna to choke down the blood it contains. Her screams turn to gurgles as the tainted blood drains down her throat.

Corbin lunges forward. "But I admitted it!" he cries. "You said—"

Roberta shrugs. "I lied. Just like you did." She turns to the guards. "Take him away. We will deal with him later." She releases Leanna, who collapses to floor, still choking. The guards try to grab Corbin, but he fights them off, baring his fangs.

"You haven't seen the last of me," he growls, before turning tail and running backstage. The guards charge after him.

Headmistress Roberta watches them go, shaking her head in dismay. Then she turns back to the audience, who's watching the scene with frightened eyes. "I'm sorry," she says, sounding tired. "Obviously there has been a change in plans. But we will regroup and meet—"

"Wait!" I interrupt. The audience looks up at me in surprise, as if to say, *There's more?* I nod my head grimly. "Corbin's not the only one who's been lying to you here."

The initiates break out into excited chatter, their eyes turning questioningly to the only other authority figure onstage: Roberta. The headmistress's face turns white.

"What do you mean, Sunny?" calls out Amber from the back.

Here goes nothing. "Look, all this time you think you've been training under the guidance of Slayer Inc.," I explain. "But what you don't know is the Alphas secretly broke off from the parent company some years ago and started their own organization. Headmistress Roberta's goal is to take over the world . . . by any means possible. You think you're defending mankind from evil vampires. But really you're just being asked to sacrifice your humanity for one person's mad lust for power."

"She's lying!" shrieks Roberta, her eyes bulging from her head. "We are on a noble crusade. Don't let this vampire sympathizer destroy you with her lies!"

"Please. If I wanted to destroy you, I would have let you drink that poisoned blood," I remind them. "Hell, it would have been a lot easier in the end. But you guys don't deserve to die. You're innocent victims being used in an otherworld power struggle. And now that you know the truth—what your fearless leaders are capable of—I hope you will step forward and take control of your own destinies."

"This is insane!" Roberta hisses. "Guards, someone, get her down from there."

"Shut up!" cries Gwen, at the back of the room. "You've had your turn to speak."

"Thank you," I say, throwing her a smile. "Look, you all have a choice here. You can allow Roberta the opportunity to steal your humanity and use you as mindless pawns for her quest for power. Or you can swap your allegiance to the real organization you signed up for. The real Slayer Inc."

The Slayers in Training cheer. Roberta reaches into her pocket and pulls out a gun. "You bitch!" she cries. "I've worked too hard on this. I'll be damned if you'll waltz in here and take it away from me now!" She aims the gun at me. But before she can pull the trigger, two of her own guards jump on her, tackling her to the ground.

It's all the slayers need. With a deafening shout, they rush forward, attacking the woman who lied to them and tried to turn them into monsters. They're so loud in their fury you can barely hear the headmistress's screams of pain as they take her down.

I grin. Once again, Sunny McDonald saves the day.

Out of the corner of my eye, I notice Jareth and Magnus have reached the altar. Jareth is scooping my sister into his arms, guiding her mouth to his wrist so she can drink his lifesaving blood. Thank God.

But we're not out of the woods yet. I glance at my watch. We're T minus ten minutes to temple bombing. "Okay, guys!" I cry. "As much as I can see you're enjoying your revenge, it's about time we get out of here." I fly over to the doorway and settle back down to the ground. "Single line and follow me. No panicking. No pushing. Pretend it's a fire drill."

As the crowd reluctantly shuffles to obey, Magnus reaches my side. He squeezes my hand in his and looks at me with smiling eyes. "You're a pretty good leader," he remarks, his voice filled with pride. "I'm going to have to bring you along more often."

I grin. "It's about freaking time you figured that out."

29

Las Vegas, Nevada

The sound of excited barking greets me as I slip backstage at the Comedy Pet Theater and push open the door that leads into the backroom. There, my heart dances with joy to find Jayden, surrounded by a happy chaos of flying fur and lolling tongues. Of course he got his job back once he returned to Vegas. After all, no one loves the animals more than he does.

"Hey," I say, sitting down beside him and pulling a big fat black cat onto my lap, stroking its sleek, shiny fur. So much better than any cat café.

"Hey, yourself," he says, then laughs as Rex tries to poke his big black nose into his pocket. "Okay, fine, fine," he says to the dog, reaching in and pulling out a biscuit. Rex barks excitedly, doing a little dance on his hind legs. Jayden throws him the treat and he catches it midair. I guess when there's this much competition from the pack you have to hone your doggie athleticism if you want to score the treats. Though from Rex's current weight, I'm guessing he's pretty successful at that.

"So how are you feeling?" I ask. "I mean, are you completely back to normal now?"

Jayden nods. "One hundred percent," he says, looking slightly bashful. "Except for the fact that somehow in the transition my hemophilia went away."

"Oh, that's amazing!" I cry.

"Yup. I can finally live a normal life without worrying about bleeding to death on a moment's notice," he says. "Which is fine by me. I've seen enough blood to last a lifetime, thank you very much."

My heart lurches. "Look, Jayden, I'm sorry . . ."

He waves me off. "You were right," he says. "I'm not cut out to be a vampire. All that action, adventure . . ." He shrugs sheepishly. "I thought I wanted all of that. That kind of glamorous lifestyle you lead. But to be honest, I'm happiest here. Just working with the dogs and cats." He smiles at me. "I'm actually thinking of opening my own shelter. Find a little farm outside the city. Take in homeless dogs and cats. Rehabilitate them. Help them become good pets for people someday."

I smile, my heart aching in my chest. "That sounds wonderful," I tell him honestly. And it does. I can't imagine ever having that. A simple life that makes me happy. Doing good for the world. Normalcy at its finest.

He studies me carefully. "Does it?" he asks. "'Cause it's not too late. You could do it with me." His eyes shine with the idea. "Just the two of us. I'd train the dogs. You could work on placing them into good homes. And you could still finish high school," he adds quickly. "I mean, whatever you want. I've got a little money put away. I could support you until you were out."

Tears well up in my eyes. "Oh, Jayden," I say. "That sounds perfect. And in another lifetime . . ." I trail off, knowing there's nothing else to say.

He nods slowly, as if he had already known my answer. Heck, he probably had. "Right," he says.

"I actually came to say good-bye," I confess. "Pyrus is furious that Magnus and I infiltrated the Alphas after he told us not to get involved. He has denounced us as traitors, using some crazy trumped-up charge, and putting a price on both of our heads. If we're found, we're going to have to stand trial for treason."

Jayden stares at me, horrified. "And if you're convicted . . . ?"

"Magnus will be staked. And I'll either be deported back to Fairyland or killed."

"But you guys did the right thing. You stopped a war. You saved innocent people."

I nod glumly. "I know. It seems like a happily ever after. Roberta and Dr. Franken in jail. The Alpha students being retrained by Slayer Inc. . . ."

"But the Consortium doesn't agree?"

"Who knows what they think? They're all too scared to speak up against Pyrus. Magnus isn't the first vampire he's kicked out of the Consortium. They're afraid if they take a stand, their vampires will suffer." I scowl. "Can you believe he still bombed the temple? Even though Magnus called him and told him he didn't have to? A beautiful historic landmark—just obliterated for no reason. Not to mention, the Holy Grail itself was still in there when it blew. I'm really glad I made you drink when I did." I shake my head, thinking of Pyrus's ugly smirk. "There's something wrong with that guy. Someone's got to get him out of power—or I'm afraid things are only going to get worse."

"So what now?"

"Jareth's still leading the Blood Coven, which is something, I guess. Pyrus doesn't know he helped us. Right now he's working on rallying the other Consortium members to our side, which is dangerous, to say the least. If Pyrus gets word of what he's doing, who knows what will happen to him . . . and the Blood Coven." I sigh. "But we've got to try."

"Oh, Sunny," Jayden cries, grabbing my hands in his. "Promise me you'll stay safe."

"I'll try my best," I say, attempting a small smile, but it's not easy.

He pulls me into a hug, squeezing me so tight it takes my breath away. The tears stream down my cheeks. When he pulls away, he searches my face with concerned eyes.

"I do love you," he says. "I know we can't be together. I understand and accept that. But I will never stop loving you. And I want you to know that."

"I know," I manage to squeak.

"And if you ever need me—for anything at all—I will be there for you. No matter what," he says firmly. "I may not be a super-strong vampire. But I am powerful in many other ways."

I try to smile. "Believe me, I know," I say. "I really do." I pause, then add, "And Jayden?"

"Yeah?"

"I care about you, too. I don't know if I should say that. I mean, it can't change how things are between us. Or the fact that I belong with Magnus. I love him and need to stick with him. But that doesn't mean my feelings for you aren't strong as hell."

His face breaks in happiness. "Oh, Sunny," he says. "That's all I ever wanted to hear." He reaches out and presses a warm hand against my cheek. It's nice to feel his humanity again. "We share a bond, you and I," he says fervently. "And no matter where we are or who we're with, that's never going to go away."

I smile at him and give him another hug. We grip onto each other so tightly it's amazing neither of us breaks in two.

"I'm not going to say good-bye," he says earnestly, finding my eyes with his own green ones. "Because I know our paths will cross again. You take care of yourself. Be safe. And tell Magnus if he lets the Consortium touch even a hair on your head he will have me to answer to." He grins shyly. "I don't care if he is a creature with supernatural powers. I'm sure somehow I could kick his ass."

I rise to my feet, my legs threatening to buckle and give way from the effort it takes. "I bet you could," I say with a small laugh as I turn to walk out of the theater and out of his life forever.

As I step out into the night, a limo pulls up to the curb. The door swings open and I scramble inside. "You okay?" Magnus asks, looking at me with worried eyes.

I shake my head, the sobs bursting out, and he pulls me to him as the driver shuts the door, rocking me in his arms as we head to the airport.

"I'm sorry," I say, trying to regain my composure.

Magnus looks at me lovingly. "Don't be," he says. "I know how hard this is for you. Leaving everything behind." He slams a fist against the leather seat. "I hate taking you away from everyone you love. I wish to God there was some other way."

"But there's not," I remind him gently. "We both know that. And I love you, Magnus. More than anything in the entire world. Where you go—I go. End of story."

"Still! All you wanted was to be normal. And I feel like I've stolen that from you . . . time and time again." He searches my face. "Are you sure you want to come with me?" he asks. "It's not going to be an easy life. And definitely not a normal one."

"Meh," I say, forcing my voice to sound breezy. "Normal is so overrated anyway."

Epilogue

Rayne

"Rayne, Rayne! Guess what, guess what? I got to level eighty!" I groggily pull the covers from over my head and squint in the early-morning (afternoon?) sunshine. Above me, my eleven-year-old half-sister, Stormy, bounces in play, an excited expression on her freckled face. Normally I don't like being woken up so abruptly, but the simple fact that I'm still alive to do it makes it a little easier to bear.

When Corbin captured me and gleefully told me of his plan to poison me and feed me to the masses like a sacrificial lamb, I figured that was just about the end of me. After all, there was no way the Consortium was going to care about one troublemaking vampire when they had the whole vampire race at stake. But I underestimated the determination of my dear, dear twin sister—who seriously is a lot more amazing than people give her credit for—single-handedly dissolving the mastermind plot without killing a single innocent. Truly genius, Sunny.

Sunny. Her name brings a blood tear to my eye. I wonder how she is. What she and Magnus are doing. They couldn't tell me where they were going, of course, in case the Consortium resorted to hypnosis or mind-control tricks to make me spill.

"Come see!" Stormy commands, grabbing my arm and trying to drag me out of bed. She, of course, doesn't know the danger Sunny's in. Her mother, Heather, told her my sister simply had to go away on a trip.

"Okay, okay!" I cry, giving in with a laugh. I crawl out of bed and allow myself to be dragged over to the computer where she's logged into World of Warcraft. It used to be my favorite video game, but lately with all that's been going on I've had little time to play it. And now my eleven-year-old stepsister has managed to out-level me.

She proudly displays her tricked-out level-eighty mage. "And look, this robe I made myself," she boasts. "It's totally leet."

I ruffle her hair. "That's awesome," I tell her. "I'm jealous."

"Do you want to play with me for a bit?" she asks, looking up at me with pleading eyes. "None of my friends are online."

I glance at my watch. Ugh. I slept later than I thought. "Sorry," I say. "I've got a training session at one. And Teifert hates when I'm late."

Stormy looks at me with admiration. "So cool." She whistles low. "I wish someday I could become a slayer like you and Mom."

"Well, study hard and maybe you will," I tease. "And play lots of WoW. I'm sure that helped me."

"Ooh, good idea!"

I say my good-byes and head through the condo and out the door. I'm meeting Mr. Teifert at the gym in a half hour. The vice president of Slayer Inc. temporarily relocated to Las Vegas so he could continue my training. Since I'm between missions, I've actually been working on getting my slayer instructor certification so I can teach other slayers or maybe even open up my own academy someday. After all, as much as I like being a vampire, after this whole experience I believe, more than ever, that our laws must be strictly enforced to avoid any potential power grabs—whether by human, vampire, or anything else.

I greet Teifert at the back room of the LA Sports Club. To my surprise he's not wearing workout gear, but a stiff three-piece suit. "Dude, what's with the outfit?" I ask. "Doesn't look like something you'll want to get blood on when I kick your butt."

But he doesn't smile at my joke. Instead he motions to a nearby set of chairs. "Sit," he instructs.

A worried feeling worms through me as I follow his instructions and take a seat. "What's going on?" I ask.

He pulls out a manila envelope from his briefcase. "The Consortium has sent out a request to Slayer Inc. An official commission."

A new assignment? "Oh-kay . . ."

"They've got a rogue vampire on the loose—one who's wanted for treason. They're asking that Slayer Inc. track him and his mate down and deliver them, undead or alive," he says. "And they're offering a large sum of money in exchange for the service."

"And you want me to carry it out?" I ask. "How much money? Are you saying I'll actually get paid this time?" I've been doing Slayer Inc.'s dirty work for so long now under the guise of "destiny." This time, I need a paycheck. Especially if I'm going to open up my little slayer school.

Mr. Teifert frowns. "Yes, there is a payment for services rendered," he says. "You'll get ten percent. One million dollars."

My eyes widen in excitement. "One million dollars? Dude! I'll take it!" I try to reach for the envelope. But Teifert locks on with a killer grip. "What?" I ask.

"Maybe you should take a look before you start cashing any checks."

"Sure, fine. Whatever. Let's see." I manage to wrestle the envelope from his hands and rip it open. Two black-and-white photos fall onto my lap.

"So let's see what naughty vampires need—" But the words die in my throat as my eyes fall on the first photo. I look up at Teifert in horror. He nods grimly.

"But . . . there's got to be some mistake!"

"No." He purses his lips. "No mistake."

"But . . . but . . ." I pick up the other photo and a mirror image of my own face stares back at me. "They want me to slay my own sister?"

~ TO BE CONTINUED ~

Turn the page for a special excerpt
from the next Blood Coven Vampire novel . . .

SOUL BOUND

Coming soon from
The Berkley Publishing Group!

"Take that, you putrid jumble-gutted zombie!" I cry, mashing my PS3 button as fast as I can, letting loose a stream of deadly bullets from my AK47 and splattering zombie brains, blood, and other assorted bodily fluids all over my bedroom television screen. The game dings as I beat my own high score once again and I lean back in my chair, feeling oh-so-satisfied. *Yeah, baby!* No one's better at Vampires vs. Zombies than me. I should enter a tournament. I'd blast all those wannabe-zombie-slaying nerds out there from here to kingdom come without even trying.

I'm about to start the bonus round when there's a knock on my door.

"Come in!" I call, hoping it's my half sister, Stormy. She's the only one who can come even close to beating me at the game and I'd love another chance to kick her eleven-year-old, video game–addicted butt.

Sure enough, the door opens and Stormy pokes her blond head into my room. "Hey, Rayne," she says. "There's some girl here to see you."

"A girl?" My mind races for possibilities, but comes up blank. I've never really been good with making girl friends in general and I'm almost positive I haven't given my home address to any mortal ones here in Vegas. (Unlike my much more social twin, Sunny, who made, like, ten friends in two days just by breathing the air at Las Vegas High School.) And, of course, no self-respecting vampire would be swinging by for a chat on a Saturday afternoon while the sun is still high in the sky. "Who?"

Stormy shrugs. "I've never seen her before," she confesses. "Though she looks a lot like the girl from *Resident Evil*."

"Video game or movie?"

"The movie. Definitely the movie."

Hmm. I'm pretty sure I'd remember making friends and influencing people who looked like Milla Jovovich . . .

"Well, send her in, I guess," I tell my sister. What the heck, right?

Stormy nods and disappears. While I'm waiting, I go and save my game. It's a little embarrassing to see the game clock pop up and realize how many hours I've been sitting in front of a television set. *But it's for a good cause,* I remind myself. After all, if Slayer Inc. received reports of me hitting the slot machines or dancing up a storm in downtown Vegas they might decide I'm not taking my whole mission to bring down my sister and her boyfriend as seriously as they'd like. Out of sight, out of mind, that's what I say. As far as they know, I'm scouring the world, one step away from my bounty.

I hear the door creak open and turn around to greet my strange visitor. Stormy isn't wrong—the girl does bear a remarkable resemblance to the famed zombie-slaughtering film star. Not only does she kind of look like her, but she dresses like her, too. I mean, it's not every day you see someone sporting a tight white tank top under a green army vest, tucked into little black shorts with garters that cling to ripped thigh-high stockings—even in Vegas. (Unless, of course, Taylor Momsen's in town . . .) The girl tops off the outfit with an amazing pair of knee-high, stack-heeled, black leather boots and two matching black leather holsters, strapped to her perfectly toned and tanned thighs.

But unlike the zombie killer of the 3-D silver screen, these holsters aren't slotted with guns. They contain stakes.

A vampire slayer. I let out a low whistle, wondering where on Earth she scored an outfit like that. Is there some kind of secret online Slayer Inc. uniform shop that sells this kind of stuff that no one told me about? I mean, I'm not all about the army vest. But those boots, man! I'd pretty much sell my soul to slip my feet into those beauties—if I hadn't already given my soul away when I first became a vampire.

Of course, I'm not entirely sure my current not-so-tanned, not-so-perfectly sculptured thighs could carry the rest of the outfit as well she does. After all, I'm still recovering from all those high-calorie blood milk shakes they force-feed you in rehab . . .

"Rayne?" the girl asks, looking down at me and removing her mirrored aviator shades. She wears a slightly disdainful look on her otherwise flawless face and I suddenly get a weird feeling I've seen her somewhere before, though for the life of me, I can't figure out where that could possibly be. "Rayne McDonald?"

"That's my name, don't wear it out," I reply automatically, feeling a little defensive. After all, she just showed up at my house, out of nowhere, giving me dirty looks like that. Even if she is the hottest thing known to slayer-kind and I'm three days overdue for a shower and wearing vampire bunny slippers instead of kick-ass boots.

She purses her obviously collagen-injected, over-glossed lips, looking at me with clear disapproval in her purple contact–covered eyes.

"Um, did you want something?" I ask, suddenly eager to get rid of her and go back to my game. After all, those brain-hungry zombies won't just explode themselves, you know.

She sighs loudly, as if she's carrying the weight of the world on her perfectly sculpted shoulders. "My name is Bertha," she says at last.

Bertha?! I burst out laughing. I'm sorry—I can't help it! This über hottie's name is Bertha? For realz? I had always assumed there was some kind of law against hot chicks being named Bertha. A name like Bertha should be reserved for girls who look like that crazy ex-vampire slayer from back home who—

Oh crap. So that's why she looks familiar . . .

"Bertha?" I cry, scrambling to my feet, trying to hide my shock. "Bertha the Vampire Slayer? Bertha the Vampire Slayer from Oakdale High School?"

Bertha had been the number-one slayer in my neck of the woods, back in the day. She had some pretty major kills to her name, too. She even bagged Lucifent, the former leader of the Blood Coven. Unfortunately, her career stalled out due to her inability to ever meet a drive-thru she didn't want to go through twice. Those pesky blood pressure issues can really put a damper on one's vampire slayer career.

But um, wow. I guess she kicked that problem . . .

"I probably look a little different than when you saw me last," she says, preening a little. I catch her glancing at her own reflection in the bedroom mirror.

I nod. I mean, holy understatement of the century, Batman! This chick did not just get her stomach stapled. She had a complete Heidi Montag makeover. Her once-pockmarked face is now porcelain-doll smooth. Her old stringy hair now flows down her back in silky waves. Her nose is at least three inches shorter and her breasts would make even Katy Perry cry.

"Wow, Bertha," I say. "You look great. Really great." And I mean it, too. Not that I'm into girls or anything. But if I was, she'd totally be first on my list.

She sniffs and I realize she's moved away from the mirror and is now giving me a critical once-over. It's then that I remember I'm currently dressed in *Nightmare Before Christmas* flannel pajamas, wearing no makeup, and haven't brushed my hair since Tuesday. At this point, I'd be dead last on pretty much anyone's list.

But still, there's no need for the judgment here. I mean, it's not like she gave me any heads-up of her impending arrival so I could apply some mascara.

"So, to what do I owe the pleasure of this visit?" I ask curiously. "I'm sure you didn't fly more than halfway across the country just to show off your extreme total makeover." Though, to be honest, if I looked like her, I'd pretty much make that my full-time job from here on out. Tracking down all those boys who once rejected me, showing off my curves . . .

"Slayer Inc. assigned me to be your new partner."

. . . finding even hotter boys and stealing them away from their cheerleader girlfriends, only to dump them after—

Wait, what?

I stare at her. "My partner?" I repeat. If my heart was still beating, it'd be slamming against my chest right about now.

She nods. "The powers that be at Slayer Inc. felt you might

need some . . . motivation . . . in tracking down your sister. So they flew me out here to assist you."

"Motivation?" I cry indignantly. "They think I have a motivation problem?" I give a loud, barking laugh at the ridiculousness of it all. A laugh that cuts short as I realize she's staring smugly at the video game screen behind me. Particularly the game clock, which is still flashing on the screen.

"Oh, that!" I wave my hand dismissively. "That's just practice. After all, you never know when you might meet up with a zombie while out on a Slayer Inc. mission. But don't worry, Berth, my girl. Can I call you Berth? I am unsurpassed at perfect head shots. Seriously, brains just start splattering all over the place at the mere sight of my mighty broomstick."

She raises an eyebrow. "That's very . . . reassuring."

I grab the remote and quickly shut off the TV. "But enough about me. Let's talk about you! What have you been up to? Are you enjoying Vegas so far? Done any gambling? You have so got to try the Krave Lounge on Fridays. Amazing Goth scene. They've got the hottest—"

"Rayne!" Bertha interrupts. "We don't have time for *clubbing*," she says, spitting out the word as if it were poison. "We're on assignment for Slayer Inc. Or perhaps you forgot?" she adds, giving the television set another look of condemnation.

I sigh. Great. And here I thought I had everything worked out so perfectly. I'd pretend to look for Sunny and Magnus and just . . . well, never find them. Sure, I'd forfeit the million-dollar bounty, but I'd forfeit a billion dollars if it meant keeping my sister safe. No big deal.

Guess Pyrus is smarter than I gave him credit for.

"Now," Bertha says, plopping down on my bed. "Let's talk

strategy. Do you have any leads? Any idea where your sister and her boyfriend might have gone?"

I shake my head. Luckily, I can give her an honest answer on that one. Don't ask, don't tell. That's my policy.

"But you're her twin. Don't you have some kind of twin ESP kind of thing? Can't you sense where she is or something?"

"The only thing I can sense is a super-annoying presence currently residing in my bedroom," I retort, annoyed at the whole twenty-questions routine and wishing she'd just go away.

She frowns. "Nice. Real nice. You think you can hurt my feelings? Cut me down and make me run sobbing from the room?" She shakes her head. "Well, sorry, sister, but this is the new and improved Bertha. And she doesn't take crap from anyone." She rises to her feet, staring directly into the mirror. "I'm back. I'm hot as hell, and I'm not going to take it anymore!"

She raises a fist in triumph, then looks at me expectantly. As if she's hoping I'll cheer on her newfound sense of self-esteem.

"Um, yay?" I try. "Go on with your bad self, you hot mama, you?"

She glares at me. "Laugh all you want," she growls. "But you won't be laughing once I have your sister and her stupid boyfriend in handcuffs." She grins wickedly.

That's it! I leap from my bed, grabbing her by her vest. "We'll see about that!"

She smirks and I realize I've walked right into her trap. "Oh, I'm sorry," she says with wide, innocent eyes. "For some reason, I thought you were supposed to be on my team. You know, the team that hired you for the job? The one that has the ability to wipe you off the face of the Earth by activating the nano-virus inside of you if you don't obey their rules?"

Argh. It takes everything I have inside to let her go. But, of course, she's right. I can't let on that I'm more interested in protecting my sister than doing my Slayer Inc. duty. After all, if I'm killed, who will protect Sunny?

Better to bide my time. Pretend to play by her rules for now. And figure out a way to beat Bertha at her own game.

"Of course," I say brightly, gritting my teeth and wishing I could just bite through that juicy little neck of hers and suck her dry. "I just meant, as a superior slayer, I'm sure to get there first."

Her lips curl into a nasty grin. "Oh, right," she says. "Of course you did." She chuckles. "But, you see, that's not going to happen either. Slayer Inc.'s given me a second chance. And I'm going to prove to them I deserve that chance. That I'm the best slayer around—no matter what I have to do." She smiles triumphantly. "Even if that means going above and beyond—and staking your sweet little sister through the heart."

JOIN THE BLOOD COVEN!

Do you want . . .
Eternal life?
Riches beyond your wildest dreams?
A hot Blood Mate to spend eternity with?

We're looking for a few good vampires! Do you have
what it takes to join the Blood Coven? Sign up online to
become a Vampire in Training, then master your skills at
Blood Coven University.

You'll go behind the scenes of the series, receive exclusive
Blood Coven merchandise, role-play with the other
vampires, and get a sneak peek at what's coming up next
for Sunny and Rayne.

BLOOD COVEN VAMPIRES
Check out all the Blood Coven Vampire titles!

Boys That Bite
Stake That
Girls That Growl
Bad Blood
Night School
Blood Ties

And don't miss the next Blood Coven Vampire novel

Soul Bound

Coming Winter 2012 from Berkley!

www.bloodcovenvampires.com
penguin.com

T125.0511